TORCHWOOD

PACK
ANIMALS

The *Torchwood* series from BBC Books:

TORCHWOOD
PACK
ANIMALS

Peter Anghelides

BBC
BOOKS

2 4 6 8 10 9 7 5 3 1

Published in 2008 by BBC Books, an imprint of Ebury Publishing
A Random House Group company

Torchwood is a BBC Wales production for BBC Television
Executive Producers: Russell T Davies and Julie Gardner

Original series created by Russell T Davies and broadcast on BBC Television
'Torchwood' and the Torchwood logo are trademarks of the
British Broadcasting Corporation and are used under licence.

The Random House Group Limited Reg. No. 954009.
Addresses for companies within the Random House Group can be found at
www.randomhouse.co.uk.

A CIP catalogue record for this book is available from the British Library.

ISBN 978 1 846 07574 2

The Random House Group Limited supports The Forest Stewardship Council
(FSC), the leading international forest certification organisation. All our titles
that are printed on Greenpeace approved FSC certified paper carry the FSC
logo. Our paper procurement policy can be found at www.rbooks.co.uk/
environment

Commissioning Editor: Albert DePetrillo
Series Editor: Steve Tribe
Production Controller: Phil Spencer

Cover design by Lee Binding @ Tea Lady © BBC 2008
Typeset in Albertina and Century Gothic
Printed in Great Britain by Clays Ltd, St Ives plc

For the Anghelides pack:
Adam, Sam, Theo, Alex and Matt.

Never animals. (Sometimes monsters.)

Light filled Father Ninian's church and lifted his soul. He loved the place most when it was like this in the mid-morning.

He shaded his eyes to stare up at the rose window above the choir loft. Its brilliant light silhouetted the music stands like skeletal overseers, and sent long shadows running down the length of the nave's nut-brown parquet. Two centuries of city building around Holy Innocents meant this was the only time of day that natural light streamed uninterrupted through any window in the eighteenth-century building. For much of Cardiff's population, passing by on their way to shops or work or clubs, the church might as well be invisible. It was tired and old, a bit like Father Ninian, but at moments like this he saw the glory of God again in its damaged pink sandstone. He could even ignore the thrumming vibration of the sewer works in the street around the corner.

He inhaled all the church's familiar smells. The snuffed smoke of extinguished offertory candles. The beeswax of polished pews. The background tang of old incense. In the vestment room there would be the scent of crisp linen and the cheap aftershave of the more senior altar boys.

7

Only boys, because Father Ninian didn't like altar girls.

Two lonely parishioners awaited his arrival for confession today. Mrs Wendle and her husband, of course, bundled in their heavy coats, sitting in the pew between the fifth and sixth Stations of the Cross. Simon of Cyrene and St Veronica gazed down with the glazed beatific expressions of nineteenth-century oils.

He genuflected before the altar. When he rose, he smiled in the Wendles' direction. Unlike the painted saints, they avoided his eyes. The pensioners preferred to talk with their priest in the supposed anonymity of the confessional, pouring out their endless personal litany of venial sins, trivial misdemeanours and perceived slights. Father Ninian kept the pain of his own mortal sins close to himself. He had entered into temptation, he knew, but the flesh was weak. He also knew the promise of damnation if his sin remained unpardoned, and that it must be expunged by sanctifying grace before the time of death. Well, he had opportunity enough for that.

His sacristan fussed by the altar rail as she prepared the church for afternoon mass. Father Ninian smiled at the old woman, and indicated the Wendles. 'The usual suspects, eh, Miss Bullivant?'

Miss Bullivant scrunched her aged mouth into a disapproving pout so that it puckered like a dog's bum. She opened the New Jerusalem Bible on the altar rail, and tapped an arthritic knuckle on a page. Father Ninian could see it was the Book of Revelation.

'Its heads were marked with blasphemous titles,' she whispered. Miss Bullivant always whispered in church. Father Ninian only ever met her in church, so perhaps she whispered all the time. 'Blasphemous titles,' she emphasised, and grasped his sleeve with a gnarled hand. An unlikely description of the Wendles, Father Ninian was about to say, when Miss Bullivant continued: 'Those youngsters play with monsters. They don't understand that Halloween should be All Hallows Eve. You should talk about it in your sermon, Father. It's not about tricks and treats and ghosts and monsters. Forget the saints, and all that's left is a cult of death.'

Father Ninian looked away from the old woman's agitated face, and studied the passive expressions of the painted saints by the Stations. 'I shall consider it, Miss Bullivant,' he said, meaning no. 'But I mustn't keep the Wendles waiting, must I? Are my vestments ready for mass?'

A guilty thought made him smile as he walked away. The pensioners might confess a mortal sin at Halloween after all. If Mrs Wendle had, in a weak moment, been practising black magic, that would be a clear transgression of the First Commandment. He could only hope.

Miss Bullivant's hiss followed him down the side aisle as she disappeared into the vestry. 'There's someone in there already. Waiting.'

Father Ninian frowned. He preferred penitents to wait outside until he had settled himself in place in the confessional box. It wouldn't do to peer too obviously through the grille. He kissed and positioned his stole, muttered his words of prayer, and said softly: 'Yes, my child?'

It sounded like a chuckle from beyond the grille. 'My child?' repeated a young man's voice.

Father Ninian hoped it wasn't another Saturday morning drunk. He leaned towards the grille. There was no smell of alcohol, just the dusty veil and the cherry-wood frame. 'How long is it since your last confession?'

'Forgive me, Father,' said the soft voice, 'for *you* have sinned.'

Now Father Ninian did peer directly through the grille. He saw a figure in an orange Cardiff United shirt. The unblinking green eyes stared back, so shockingly direct that the priest flinched away. He knew this boy. No longer a boy, of course, he was… who? Father Ninian's mind reeled as he tried to compose his thoughts. One of his altar servers from… eight years ago, perhaps more. Gary or Gareth or Graeme. Gareth, it was Gareth. Must be in his twenties now. How could he have forgotten Gareth?

'You're not going to forgive me,' Gareth said coldly.

Father Ninian fiddled with his trouser leg. He couldn't leave now, he'd barely been in here two minutes, what would the Wendles think? 'It's not me who forgives you, my son. I absolve you in the name of—'

'I don't want your absolution.'

'You could have sought penance at any church. Why choose Holy Innocents?'

'Holy Innocents?' Another snort of laughter. 'You're not wholly innocent yourself, are you, Father?' He rattled the partition between them. 'I've brought you this.'

A piece of coloured card was pushed through the side of the grille. It was like a large playing card, the size of a paper sheet folded in half. Father Ninian plucked it from the frame and studied it quizzically. His question died on his lips when he heard the fizzing noise, like a match being struck. Absurdly, the priest's first thought was of Health and Safety regulations that forbade smoking inside the building but still allowed his altar boys to light a thurible and wave incense around the church.

A bright flare of illumination filled the confessional. The

priest felt his heart pound. The place was ablaze with light. In the confined space, a squat human shape was forming before his eyes, dark against a brilliance brighter than the rose window.

No, not a human. Now he could see a monster in human form. Rags loosely covered its creased leathery hide. A skein of scraggy hair tufted around a snarling face of deep-set eyes and drooling mouth. Its forehead was marked with deep wrinkles, brutal furrows scribbled across its brow. The enclosed space filled with its foul stench.

'Oh God!' cried Father Ninian.

'As usual,' said Gareth's calm voice, 'God has nothing to do with it.'

Father Ninian choked a scream. The creature cocked its hideous head and turned its attention to him. It seized him in one savage movement and raked the flesh of his face and neck with its sharp teeth. The priest shrieked and slipped from its grasp. He squirmed between its straddling legs, through the curtain, and out onto the parquet of the aisle. Mrs Wendle craned her neck out of her overcoat, and stared down at him like a startled turtle.

Inside the confessional, the monster lurched to left and right in a furious attempt to escape from its wooden prison. The curtain wrenched aside and the creature loomed in the frame, bellowing. The Wendles fled.

Father Ninian scrambled backwards down the side aisle, too terrified to decide whether to waste time trying to stand. The creature slammed two pews aside. Beyond it, the priest could see Gareth swiftly but calmly walking away into the shadows at the rear of the church.

'Gareth, help me!' pleaded Father Ninian.

Gareth's orange football shirt continued to move away.

The young man's calm voice floated back in the church's echo. 'Help you? I can't even forgive you.'

Just as Father Ninian reached the altar rail, the monster reached Father Ninian.

ONE

Banana Boat was driving Rhys Williams crazy. Rhys hated shopping trips at the best of times, and his long-time school friend's relentlessly cheerful running commentary during their progress through the out-of-town mall was wearing him down. That parking was impossible, said Banana. These food court prices were a rip-off, announced Banana. Those lasses in Valley Girl were well shaggable, declared Banana. And is that kid wearing a Halloween mask, or does being that ugly come naturally?

He'd been hyper since getting back from Lanzarote. Rhys was almost sorry that the Spanish authorities had released Banana from his brief stay in police custody. He'd been caught flogging bootleg CDs in Tias, but unexpectedly allowed home with just a warning. 'They kept my bloody CDs, though,' Banana had grumbled, to Rhys's incredulity.

The way today was going, he'd be behind bars again before lunch, they wouldn't have the wedding coats hired, and they'd both miss this evening's international at the Stadium to boot.

'Hello?' called Banana from the nearby changing room. He

was poking his head around the curtain and trying to attract the blonde assistant's attention. 'Can you help me, love? The toilet roll has run out in here.'

Rhys struggled not to smile. The badge on the blonde's bosom told Rhys that she was senior sales assistant Kelly. The prices in the catalogue told Rhys that his dad wasn't going to get any change out of his wedding budget.

'Sorry about him,' muttered Rhys. 'He's my best man.' Senior sales assistant Kelly's tight smile made him wonder ruefully whether he'd made the wrong choice of best man. He'd considered the alternatives. Dozy Daf? Barry 'Island' McGinn with the stutter? No, on reflection, Banana was the least-worst man.

Rhys signed away a month's salary as a deposit, and dragged Banana Boat out of the store. A group of four teenagers swaggered past, identikit grey hoods pulled up in defiance of the mall's rules, and indifferent to the wake they caused in the crowd of shoppers. What was it about you lumpen hooligans, he wanted to ask, swaggering about like a pack of animals? Rhys clicked his tongue, but held it too; he could already imagine Gwen admonishing him, and she was a police officer who supposedly knew how to handle the little monsters. And she knew how to handle real, big monsters too, of course. That put things into perspective for him.

Banana leaned on the rail, peering down into Pendefig Mall like a fisherman surveying prospective catches.

'It's madness,' Banana told him. 'You said it would be quieter out here. Should have gone to Evans the Suit in town, like your dad said.'

'Evans Suit Hire,' Rhys corrected him.

'Suit yourself,' laughed Banana.

Rhys studied the till receipt from senior sales assistant Kelly. Too late for that option.

The escalators were crammed with overloaded shoppers, and the ground-floor walkway below seemed to quiver as snaking currents of people moved ceaselessly in their Saturday morning quest to consume.

'Should have stayed in town,' insisted Banana.

Rhys shook his head. 'That'll be worse. Especially when the football crowds start arriving at the stations.'

Banana wasn't listening. He was pointing indiscreetly at the lower level. 'Is that Sheelagh Thompson? God, I could drop a peanut into her cleavage from here. In fact, there's room for the whole packet.'

'You big kid. What are you, twelve?' Rhys groaned.

'I know,' grinned Banana, showing his even white teeth, 'I'm an animal. But she's my type. I fancy a bit of blond on blonde. Just 'cause *you're* getting married, sad boy, doesn't mean the rest of us have stopped doing road tests.' He gazed almost pleadingly at Rhys.

Rhys looked at his watch. It felt like they'd been here hours, but it was still only half past ten. 'I think I can get the rest of the stuff myself, Banana. Why don't you knock off now, and I'll meet you later at the match?'

Banana's grin got even wider. 'If Gwen'll let you.' He pressed one thumb into the open palm of his other hand. 'Like that, you are, mate! Don't get caught!'

'You can bloody talk!' Rhys called after him. 'Why not buy yourself some CDs while you're here?'

Banana flicked a cheery V-sign over his shoulder as he strode off to the escalator, irresistibly drawn by Sheelagh Thompson's tits.

Rhys had to keep an eye out. He'd promised Gwen he

wouldn't shop here today. It was unlucky to see the dress beforehand, she'd told him. He'd said that was only if she was wearing it, and she'd retorted that she was planning on trying it on first, thank you, and he should keep well out of the way. Somewhere else in the Pendefig Mall, she and that mate of hers from school, Megan, would be in one of the bridal-wear shops and spending a small fortune. So he could get this done, and still be back home in time to cook lunch, as he'd promised.

Rhys pulled a crumpled scrap of paper from his jeans pocket. He could leave the bridesmaids' gifts for another time, but he had time to get a present for the least-worst man before he sneaked off home again.

He made his way up the escalator, nudging past the standing pedestrians on the right. As Rhys stepped off the moving stairway, a matronly woman beside him told her daughter proudly: 'That there is the biggest shoe shop in South Wales. And *I* know the manager!' Gwen would have loved that one – he'd have to remember it later.

Several angry shouts from the opposite escalator made Rhys twist around. A ripple worked its way down the line as someone shoved roughly past. Another kid in a hurry. Round-shouldered in his leather jacket, and wearing a stupid Halloween mask. Most of the bumped shoppers shrugged, fuming inside but too frightened to speak up. One old codger at the bottom was having none of it, though. Rhys watched in amusement from his position near the top of the opposite escalator. The old guy raised his furled umbrella and gave the kid a whack across the arm. The kid paused briefly to snarl through his mask. The old guy recoiled as though he'd been spat at, but gave the kid another smack with his brolly.

'Ooh, that's gotta smart!' breathed Rhys in appreciation.

The kid hunched his shoulders, and loped off into the crowd of shoppers, knocking aside those who didn't make way as he barged through. From the hand gestures they were making, it was clear the kid smelled none too good, either. Dirty, uncouth little yob.

The upper level had a row of toyshops. Where better, mused Rhys, to buy a joke gift for Banana, the big kid? If he couldn't find something here, there were always the market stalls outside the mall's main entrance.

The first two stores were for pre-school and infants, brightly lit and devoid of customers. In the far corner, though, was a smaller toyshop. This one had a hand-painted sign fixed precariously above the uPVC frame of its standard mall store front: Leonard's Toys and Games. And, unlike the other stores, it seemed to be full of chattering kids. The front window was decked out in shades of orange and black, crammed with Halloween pumpkins, witches' cloaks and hats, vampire teeth and wolf-man masks, liberally sprayed with stringy lines of cobweb.

Inside, old-fashioned wall shelving was stacked with board games and fantasy novels. Rhys saw no electronic games. Rotating wire racks were hung with blister packs of carved models, mythical characters that included gorgons, winged serpents, a Cyclops. The thin-faced shopkeeper smiled at Rhys as he meandered through the closely stacked displays.

There was a whoop from the rear of the shop. A group of young adults had crowded around a hand-crafted landscape. They positioned characters, painted versions from the blister packs, in competing formations. Each participant held a hand of brightly coloured, oversized playing cards. A rangy lad with spiked hair rattled dice from a cup. Whatever he scored, it caused another deep-throated cheer of encouragement from the crowd. Rhys could feel their energy coursing through the cluttered shop. 'Geek power,' he murmured.

He blenched as he almost walked into a figure by the tills. It was an old shop dummy, a reclaimed version of the sort you'd find in big department stores like Wendleby & Son. Its incongruously elegant hands poked out from the neatly pressed boiler suit, and a scowling full-face mask obscured most of its sculpted head. Rhys had jumped involuntarily because he recognised the tufted hair, deeply furrowed brow, and angular foam teeth. It was so like that creature he'd seen in the Torchwood dungeon. What had Gwen called it? 'A Weevil,' he said.

'It's a Toothsome, actually,' said the shopkeeper. 'From MonstaQuest?' Rhys looked blankly at him. 'I'm forever "translating" for parents. It's the new trading-card game. Models and masks too, you know.' Rhys obviously looked like he didn't. 'Bit of a craze with the older teens and upwards. Doing really well.' The shopkeeper's smile looked like a mouthful of baby teeth. He was younger than Rhys. Unshaven, with dark uncombed hair. Eager. 'Are you buying for your kids?'

Rhys laughed. 'No kids. Not yet,' he said, and wondered why he'd added that.

He remembered what Banana had said before he left: 'I'm a monster.' Yes, these would do. And the joke was even better for him and Gwen, because they knew real monsters when they saw them.

'MonstaQuest, eh?' Rhys pulled a scrunched-up tenner from his pocket. 'I'll take a pack of those, then.'

The shopkeeper had just handed Rhys the oversized cards when the mall's fire alarm went off.

TWO

'Come on, Ianto, get a move on,' said Jack Harkness. He wriggled in the driver's seat of the SUV. 'My ass is going to sleep here.'

'I know,' muttered Ianto Jones. 'I heard it snoring.' He tapped some more at the compact keyboard and the heads-up display flickered its response. 'Believe me, I'm as keen to get out of this vehicle as you are. Some date, huh?'

'There's still time, we'll be there,' soothed Jack. 'Place won't be open yet.' He peered through the grimy windscreen at the grey office buildings. A handsome guy in ugly brown clothes was approaching down the narrow pavement. 'He'd look better out of that suit,' noted Jack.

Handsome Guy had to squeeze past the side of the SUV. He gave them a grim stare. Jack grinned right back. 'What's his problem? I put the parking indicators on, didn't I?'

'They're supposed to be hazard warning lights,' admonished Ianto. The regular noise of the indicators continued their tut of disapproval. 'No, the Rift signature has dropped off. Big surge, died right back, not a trace now. Whatever it was has gone.'

Jack was only half-listening. He had adjusted the electronic wing mirror to follow Handsome Guy's progress down the pavement. He watched the man lose his temper with a Maestro parked so far onto the pavement that its wing mirror prevented anyone passing. The pedestrian stalked back around the front of the car and hammered on the bonnet with his fist. This made the occupant lean forward to wave him away. That's when Jack recognised the driver.

'Oh, not today, please!'

Jack clicked off the hazards, twisted the ignition, and drove smoothly into traffic. The Maestro reversed back from the alarmed pedestrian, and swerved around him into the roadway.

Ianto bounced uncomfortably in the passenger seat. 'What is it?'

'That radio journalist again,' Jack replied, flicking a look at the rear-view mirror. 'David Brigstocke.' The Maestro was half a street back, so he took a sharp right. 'I'm not good on small talk.'

'Tell me about it,' replied Ianto.

'So let's see if I can shake him *and* track that last big surge in the Rift signature.'

Ianto was already pattering away on his keyboard. The heads-up display altered to show a road schematic and a recommended route. Ianto winced as Jack scraped the wheels against the kerb. A puddle sluiced across the nearest office wall.

Jack took a racing right-hand turn across traffic. 'These brakes feel a little spongy,' he noted, 'Did you get them serviced?'

'Didn't have the parts,' replied Ianto, 'so I made the horn louder instead. Take this left.'

A cyclist swerved, crashed, and cursed.

Jack glared at Ianto. 'One-way street?'

Ianto smiled. 'Seems to work in both directions.'

A minute later the SUV slewed to a halt, parked across double yellows in a side street.

Jack and Ianto stepped out into the main carriageway. It was flanked by office buildings. The sour stink of drains told Jack there were sewer repairs further down the street long before he saw the candy-stripe tarpaulin of the covered work area. A young man with an equally sour expression ran past them and away, his orange football shirt the brightest spot in the grey street. He was presumably escaping the stench as quickly as possible.

Ianto covered his nose with a dark red handkerchief. It matched his dark red shirt, of course, Jack noted. 'There's a church.' Ianto held his PDA out to Jack.

Incongruously slotted between two office buildings was the narrow sandstone façade of an eighteenth-century place of worship. 'Holy Innocents,' explained Ianto. 'Sometimes called the Concealed Church of Cardiff.'

'I've seen better-concealed churches,' said Jack, and started up the short flight of steps to the main entrance. 'This was the high spot for the Rift activity?'

A shrill scream from inside the building curtailed Ianto's reply. He pocketed the PDA, and followed Jack up the steps at a run.

They were both caught by surprise as the church's double oak doors sprang open. Jack stumbled into the handrail by the steps, and Ianto sprawled onto the pavement.

The Weevil that had burst through the doors blinked hard in surprise. It fended off the sudden brightness with desperate swipes of its taloned hands. It sniffed the air.

Jack fumbled for his disabling spray, but the creature was off down the street before his hand was out of his coat. 'Check out the church,' he snapped at Ianto, and hared off after the Weevil.

The chase proved futile. The Weevil's lolloping gait swiftly took it to the smelly repair works. Once it had dived into the brightly coloured canvas tent, Jack knew it was already lost to the sewer system.

And besides, David Brigstocke had just stepped forward from a nearby side street. Jack recognised the same old check jacket, this time over battered pale blue jeans. Maybe they didn't pay radio journalists enough for decent clothes. Maybe clothes weren't important on the radio.

Jack put his hands on his hips and huffed, a combination of catching his breath and snorting with exasperation. 'Put that thing away,' he told Brigstocke. 'I'm in no mood to talk.'

Brigstocke smiled his thin smile, and pocketed the digital recorder. 'Would it matter, Captain Harkness? When I played back our last conversation, it had mysteriously changed into a recording of Radio Five Live.'

'Tuning problem,' said Jack.

'Torchwood problem,' responded Brigstocke smoothly. He was using his 'on-air' voice, the slightly clipped Swansea intonation familiar to *Cardiff Tonight*'s thousands of listeners. 'Talk to me, Jack.'

'Busy day,' said Jack, and walked back to the church. 'And I'm working.'

'So am I, Captain Harkness.' Brigstocke scuttled along behind him, trying to look in control and so resisting the urge to run. 'You know what happened to my mate Rhodri. And it's not like there aren't plenty of other people who've seen what Torchwood get up to. Police, Ambulance, Army.

You're first on the scene, first to leave. You were there that day with Rhodri… I have corroborating evidence.'

He hissed his insistence as they entered the church. The calm interior seemed to demand it. And it also meant that a soft keening became audible at the far end of the church.

Jack found Ianto sitting in the front pew and comforting an old woman. She must have been in her eighties, unless the experience had aged her. The torn remains of a man, wrapped in the shredded remnants of priest's clothing, were scattered by the vestry door.

'Miss Bullivant is the sacristan. She found the body.' With the old lady clutching him, Ianto affected to be unable to pocket his PDA, so he passed it up to Jack. 'I've already called the police.' Jack saw that Ianto's real motive was to show him the Rift analysis on the display, relayed from Toshiko back at the Hub.

Brigstocke slumped into the next pew back, trying not to look at the corpse. He was saying 'Oh God' repeatedly. When he caught Jack's eye, he stopped fumbling with his handheld recorder, and put it away again. 'It's enough to shake your faith in God,' he mumbled. He watched as Ianto carefully disentangled himself from the old woman. 'He's gone to a better place,' Brigstocke added feebly.

Jack leaned in. 'That the best you can offer?' he breathed.

Brigstocke flushed angrily. 'This was one of those creatures wasn't it?' he whispered urgently. 'Don't deny it, I have—'

'Corroborating evidence,' said Jack. 'Yeah, I'm sure.'

'And that dreadful smell. It's like the sewer.'

Jack grinned cruelly. 'Did your corroborating evidence show these creatures are copraphagic?'

'They're what?'

Ianto accepted his PDA back from Jack. 'They eat faeces.'

23

Jack enjoyed the disgust on Brigstocke's face. 'What, you're a journalist and you didn't know that?'

'We have dictionaries.'

'You know that's not what I meant.'

Miss Bullivant had risen and gone to the altar rail. She was looking at a Bible, one trembling hand pressed against her mouth. The book was spattered with the dead man's blood. Jack could just make out the words she was reading: 'I saw that one of its heads seemed to have had a fatal wound but that this deadly injury had healed.' The old woman was sobbing now.

The parquet floor by the body was dark and slick with blood. Jack trod carefully over to the body. Nothing much to pursue here, the ugly but familiar aftermath of a Weevil attack. The scratched trail from the body to the crooked remnants of the confessional box gave the narrative for the priest's final moments. One arm was bitten almost clean off.

And clutched in the left hand was a large, colourful playing card. Jack checked that Brigstocke was occupied by the sacristan. When he plucked the card out of the priest's grasp, he had to tug it from clawed fingers. Cadaveric spasm, wasn't that how Owen described it? Torchwood saw more of it than any scene-of-crime officers, that rare pre-rigor stiffening from intense emotion during violent death.

The card was about A5-size. Stiff, though not as stiff as the priest. The back of it had a bright logo that read: MonstaQuest. The front showed a stylised cartoon monster, with attributes rating it on different scales: Age, Height, Weight, Savagery, Intelligence.

Brigstocke glared at Jack. 'First on the scene…' said Brigstocke.

'First to leave,' concluded Jack. 'Come on, Ianto.'

'Who's he,' grumbled Brigstocke, 'your boyfriend?'

'Yeah,' grinned Jack. 'And we're late for our date. Never mind, David, you found your story for this evening. Brutal murder of local priest. You got an eyewitness. Make sure you take good care of her.'

The sacristan clutched Brigstocke's forearm. He was clearly in a dilemma about leaving her there. '*You're* never going to be a witness, are you, Jack?' The journalist raised his voice for the first time. The echo followed Jack and Ianto out of the church.

In the SUV, Jack passed the MonstaQuest card to Ianto.

'Good likeness,' said Ianto, turning the card over in his hand. 'But what's a Toothsome?'

THREE

The wedding dress wasn't ready. Gwen Cooper sat calmly in the food court while bridesmaid Megan got angry on the bench beside her. 'It's an outrage, is what it is,' Megan snapped. 'How do you know it'll even be ready in time for the wedding? Worst thing that could happen.'

'The way you're going on, you'd think this was *your* wedding dress!' Gwen sipped her cappuccino and smiled. She could think of lots of worse things, including yesterday evening's encounter with Ianto, a slime creature, and a mop and bucket. But none that she could tell Megan about. 'C'mon, let's make the most of it. We can look for my going-away outfit. There's a sale on in Happy, I saw signs in the window.' She checked her watch: nearly half ten. 'We might still beat the rush.'

Megan looked liked she'd prefer to go back into Best Day Bridal and tear another strip off the unfortunate manageress.

Gwen rubbed Megan's arm. 'Mum insisted I get something special. "Don't want that snooty cow Brenda sniping as your car leaves for the airport" is how she put it.' She knew Megan could be jollied out of her mood by a good grumble about Rhys's formidable mum. Soon to be Gwen's formidable mother-in-law.

'Don't like this place,' announced Megan as they negotiated a path through the mid-morning rush of Pendefig Mall shoppers. 'Flowers are all fake. Never a bin when you need one. The toilets are miles away on the top floor. And the place is heaving with bloody English students this time of year.'

'What about Southampton Simon you went out with? He was a post-grad, wasn't he?'

'Exactly,' said Megan with a finality that brooked no further argument. She popped her head up above the crowd, like a meerkat. 'There, what about Valley Girl? They had some fantastic Vivienne Westwood jackets.'

Shoppers were looking to the opposite side of the mall. Shouting and a ripple of people down the escalator indicated someone shoving his way down. Gwen fought the temptation to go over – she was emphatically off-duty, and now was not the time for a spot of community policing. She followed Megan. When she tucked her handbag firmly under her arm, she could feel the butt of her Torchwood handgun. Off-duty, maybe, but never off-guard.

'I am loving your boots, by the way.' Megan appraised Gwen's black, calf-length footwear. 'Converse?'

'Belstaff,' admitted Gwen.

'God!' shrieked Megan. 'They pay you well enough in Special Ops, then. How much?'

Gwen didn't like to admit how much she'd spent on them. She hadn't told Rhys yet. 'They're a bit of a bugger after a couple of hours,' she admitted. 'Wearing them because I want to make sure the jacket will go-with, you see.'

'How about this? It's waisted, apparently.' Megan picked

out a tailored anthracite jacket. 'Just the thing for the hen night, eh?' she brayed. 'We'll all be wasted.'

Gwen held the jacket against herself. It was the sort of thing she'd have bought without a second thought before she joined Torchwood. Now she found herself considering the practicalities of washing alien grime out of designer gear. Nothing with 'Dry-Clean Only' these days, if she could help it.

'It says "Anglomania" on the label.' Megan sucked her cheeks in. 'Lovely thing, though. So I won't tell Rhys if you won't.'

Gwen slipped on the jacket and examined her reflection in a tall mirror. She politely declined Megan's offer to hold her bag, instead putting her foot on the strap. 'Does this make my arse stick out? And if you can't be kind, Megan, at least have the decency to be vague.'

Megan cackled. 'I used to say that to Banana Boat. Not that he took the hint.' She affected to remove a piece of lint from the arm of Gwen's jacket. 'Is he back in the country?'

'Missing him?'

'Like a hole in the head.' Megan wrinkled her nose. 'That was a bigger mistake than Dr Simon.'

'Or Geraint Honess.'

Megan groaned theatrically. 'Still, if I had those three in front of me and a shotgun with two barrels, know who I'd kill and who I'd spare?' She cocked her head to one side, but didn't wait for Gwen's answer. 'I'd shoot that idiot Banana twice, to be completely sure.'

'And then smash his head with the stock!' laughed Gwen.

'Stock? Listen to you,' noted Megan.

Gwen looked away. 'Firearms training,' she muttered.

Megan's mood seemed to have brightened, though.

'Anyway, this isn't a shotgun wedding is it. Is it?' she asked again teasingly.

Gwen didn't respond. Through the open frame of the shop doorway, something outside had caught her eye. An all-too familiar hunched shape in a leather jacket was shoving through the crowd, spitting and snarling.

'Stay here,' Gwen said. She picked up her bag and ran through the exit and towards the Weevil.

'You clumsy bastard!' snapped Jenny Bolton. 'I'll have you.' The yob had barged into her, and spun her into an old woman tugging a wheeled shopping basket. Jenny had been in the middle of phoning her mum, to find out where she had got to. The phone was a birthday present from her mum. So where was she? Supposed to be outside Boots a quarter of an hour ago. Jenny wasn't going to wait all day, was she?

The yob was still shoving his way through the crowd ahead of her with an odd sort of lolloping walk. He careered into a gaggle of teenagers who were entering Valley Girl. A burly goth with long black hair and startling kohl eyes grabbed the yob by the lapels of his leather jacket. 'Watch it, mate,' said the goth slowly and calmly. 'Other people here. Can't you see through that mask?' Other shoppers seemed unsure whether to stare or look away in embarrassment, avoiding involvement. Not Jenny. She fumbled with her phone's camera setting. Take a photo, get him banned. Fed up of being knocked about.

What was wrong with him, anyway? All that scrubby pale hair, could be alopecia. Or chemo. Jenny had momentary second thoughts about the photo. Then the yob gave a weird guttural roar and lunged at the goth, head-butting him. The goth yelled, tumbled backwards, blood on his face.

The yob whirled round, sweeping his surroundings with a roar. It was a horribly realistic mask – red-eyed, drooling, and now flecked with blood. Jenny's thumb jerked, almost involuntary, on the shutter button. The flash flickered, the yob threw up a clawed hand.

'Gotcha,' said Jenny. Except she hadn't. She'd been distracted by the camera flash, and the yob must have slipped away into the crowd.

A young woman skidded to a halt beside her. Long black hair, straight-cut fringe, bit of a wild look in her eyes. Nice jacket, noticed Jenny, but the security tag was still on the sleeve. That would explain the beeping alarms. An angry blond lad – blue Valley Girl shirt, pink face – grabbed her shoulder. The dark-haired woman delved into her handbag and brandished an ID at him: 'Leave it. I'm Gwen Cooper, with the police.'

'Police don't shoplift,' snapped the angry lad. His pink face paled when Gwen Cooper replaced her ID with a handgun.

A space appeared in the crowd. Gwen Cooper closed her free hand over Jenny's phone and shut it so that Jenny couldn't photograph her. 'Did you see where it went?'

Jenny shook her head mutely.

The armed woman was fishing something else out of her bag. Too small to see what, but she was poking it into her ear with her finger. 'Tosh,' she was saying now. But anything else was lost in another shattering roar behind her.

Two more yobs smashed through the nearby fire doors and charged their way through the crowd. A strong blast of cold air gusted through the mall behind them. Newspapers and leaflets whirled and spun. Shoppers tumbled aside, sprawled onto the floor, their bags bursting and the contents scattering. Several people howled in shock and pain as the masked hooligans forced their way past. Screams mixed with the howl of the wind. There were tears and blood. The yobs slashed at people with knives, like talons in their hands. The crowds shrank back as the yobs shoved past and fled for the exit doors.

A wall of cowering shoppers shied backwards, inadvertently pressing Jenny against the plate glass of Valley Girl. A stiletto scraped her instep, a damp umbrella pressed against her face. She could hear the glass behind her creaking. Panicked, Jenny jabbed with her elbows and shuffled sideways as best she could. She managed to squirm off the window and practically fell through a pair of fire doors.

Jenny staggered into an echoing space of cold air. These were the emergency stairs. The fire doors had swung closed. She peered through their tall, narrow windows and saw the crowd was still thronged outside. No way past, so she decided to take the stairs and cut across the upper floor instead.

On the next landing she found a torn leather coat. Further up the stairway was the slumped body of another yob, still wearing his face mask. Had he fallen? Maybe he was drunk. He smelled as though he'd shat himself. Jenny ventured closer. 'You all right there?'

There was so much blood. One of the figure's arms had been torn off. The arteries had sprayed out over the stairs and up the wall. She could see that it wasn't a person, more like a savage ape. Who would dress an animal up like that yob in the mall? She still had her phone in her hand, so she checked the picture she'd taken – the creature was unmistakably the same. In the confusion before, she must have forwarded it to her mum. Her mum was returning the call.

Jenny whimpered as she pressed Receive. Then she shrieked as the fire alarm went off.

The clamour disturbed something else in the stair well. Jenny hadn't noticed it where it had spread itself on the underside of the stairs. A hellish bat-like creature dropped in front of her, the size of a large dog. It surveyed her with pitiless, pitch-black eyes.

The phone dropped from her hands and skittered down the stairwell. Jenny's desperate thought was: 'If I've broken that phone, my mum'll kill me.'

But it wasn't her mum that killed Jenny Bolton.

Gwen couldn't understand where the abrupt rush of air was coming from. Even if they'd opened loading doors somewhere, it shouldn't whip up this kind of through current. She cupped her left hand awkwardly over her right ear. 'I can barely hear you, Tosh. Get back-up to Pendefig Mall. I got two uncontained Weevils, and it's a mess.'

'I said, I thought it was your day off,' shouted Toshiko. 'Anyway, back-up isn't available.'

Gwen pursued the fleeing Weevils away from Valley Girl and through the yelling crowds, unable to take a shot for fear of hitting a terrified bystander. Most of the shoppers jumped aside, and those that didn't were slashed by the Weevils. Gwen couldn't remember seeing these alien creatures in crowds like this before. Maybe that was what had spooked them. The ugly brutes kept glancing over their shoulders as they tore through the mall. Eventually they must have spotted natural light from the glass entrance doors that led out into the street, and their pace increased.

She half-considered abandoning her expensive boots, because the heels made chasing at full pelt quite difficult. But by the time she'd tugged them off her feet, the Weevils would be long gone.

The fire alarm went off, startlingly loud. A new ripple of uncertainty ran through the crowd.

The Weevils slammed into the glass doors on the hinge edges, and bounced off. Gwen took careful aim at the nearest one, but her target was obscured by a woman running across her line of fire. Gwen stepped calmly aside and refocused. But the Weevils had given up their brief assault on the exit. A fire door opened in the flanking wall. The Weevils leaped for the gap, knocking aside a startled janitor whose dropped bucket clattered down the steps after them.

'Bloody hooligans!' he bellowed after them. Further remonstrations died in his throat as Gwen squeezed past him, her gun ready.

The stairs led to the service area in the basement. In the blissful absence of screaming shoppers, the loudest noises were the hum of equipment and the insistent clamour of the fire alarm. Even the sound of rushing wind was replaced with the whine of air-conditioning systems. Gwen could finally hear Toshiko yelling at her through her earpiece. 'OK, you're very loud and clear now, Tosh.' Her own soft voice echoed oddly in the concrete stairwell.

Toshiko's voice crackled in her ear again. 'I'm on my way.'

'Who's looking after the shop?'

'I've left the pet in charge.'

'Does a pterodactyl know how to answer a phone?' hissed Gwen.

'Pteranodon,' retorted Toshiko.

'Yeah, that'd make a difference. What about everyone else?'

'Jack's out in Newport with Ianto. Checking out Rift activity.'

'Is that what they're calling it now?'

'Suspicious peak in the readings around a church,' continued Toshiko. 'And Owen's doing that hotel investigation. So it's just you and me. See you soon.'

The connection dropped.

Gwen continued down the cold, grey-painted steps. Smears of blood on the walls showed where the Weevils had pressed against them on their headlong flight down the stairs.

The lighting in the maintenance corridor hummed overhead. One fluorescent tube with a faulty starter struggled to come on, sparking its fitful illumination. Gwen tried to get her bearings. If Toshiko had been there, she'd have called up a schematic of the mall on her PDA and picked out their precise location with GPS. Gwen didn't have the time to get her PDA out of her handbag, never mind work out how to interface it to the mall's wireless network. From what she remembered of the sloping ground where Pendefig was built, this maintenance corridor below the main shopping area would lead out into the rear of the mall and the loading areas.

In a pool of light fifty metres ahead, one of the Weevils had stopped. It hunched down against a wall, quivering. Beneath it was a crumpled body. Another human victim, thought Gwen, a hot flush of anger suffusing her. Killed and eaten by the alien. No matter how many victims she'd seen since joining Torchwood – and it must have been dozens – she was determined never to get hardened to this. She'd known mates in the police who joked about the street detritus that they encountered, like they were objects and not people. They'd be shaken out of their cold indifference, she thought, if they'd seen how animals from other worlds really did treat humans like bags of meat. And then they might have a bit more respect even for Queen Street's stinking vagrants or Friday night drunks slumped outside the Adonis Bar.

The Weevil was shaking its head slowly over the body. It wasn't eating, it was mourning. The body in its arms was the other Weevil. Gwen almost laughed as she trained her gun on it. The surviving Weevil was trying to make itself look small, even in plain view. Did it think she wouldn't see it?

It wasn't hiding from her, though. It was now staring, terrified, at something opposite.

Another creature squatted just inside the overlapping plastic doors of a storage area. Gwen saw its breath steaming the cloudy, scratched plastic.

Abruptly, it lunged through the doors. The Weevil flinched, but did not flee. It was transfixed to the spot, or resigned to its fate. The attacker plunged its bestial face into the Weevil's neck and shook it like a dog with a toy. The Weevil let out one pitiful, high-pitched squeal before sagging against the wall.

Gwen choked in horror. And the attacking creature immediately snapped its head up in her direction. It was the size of a Labrador. Its scaly black body had strong rear limbs. When it spread its thin, powerful forearms, the attached wings spread incongruously large either side of its tiny, savage head. Coal-dark eyes glittered in the light of the corridor, and it hissed a sibilant warning breath from a mouth wide with savage teeth. With the wings extended, it looked like a bizarre bat.

The powerful back legs shivered. Gwen had seen her mum's cat do that as it prepared to leap at a bird in the garden.

Gwen feinted to her right. As the bat sprang, Gwen loosed off two quick shots in succession, and fell left.

The creature shrieked an echoing cry as both bullets tore through its wing. It continued its run, scraping past her and heading towards the exit ramp at the end of the grey corridor. Gwen launched herself after it, firing twice more at its back.

She burst out from the top of the exit ramp, squinting into the bright morning light, nerves jangling in anticipation of the bat-creature waiting for her. Instead, it was flapping around in a circle, unable to fly off and hemmed in by parked delivery vehicles. Its unforgiving black eyes bored into her, but it was going nowhere.

No more options.

Gwen adjusted her firing stance, feet at shoulder-width, left foot advanced, leaning slightly forward, right elbow almost straight. It had become instinct now, and she rarely had the need, or the luxury of time, to think it through.

She took a breath, and prepared to exhale half of it before she fired the round.

A lightning flash from the middle distance dazzled her. A streak of yellow-white light spiralled around the bat-creature, enveloping it and then dissipating.

Gwen whirled, half-fearing that the monster had got round her. But there was no noise from the ramp behind, nor any movement under the haphazardly parked transit vans nearby. High on a pole, a CCTV camera turned lazily towards her position, as though mocking her.

There was nothing for either of them to see. The creature had vanished.

The emergency vehicles speckled the market stalls with blue light. Traders were hurriedly bundling their goods into cardboard boxes or sheets as the crowds flooded out of the mall and into their pitches on the street. Empty plastic punnets scrunched underfoot in the spilled remnants of a fruit and veg stall, overturned in the evacuation. Gwen could hear Toshiko chattering in her right ear. Something about parking. Megan grumbled beside her into her left.

'Madness it was,' Megan babbled. 'The air conditioning went crazy. There was clothes blowing all over the place. We got out through the emergency exit at the back of Valley Girl.'

'We?'

'Me and Robert.' She thumbed a gesture towards the pink-faced lad nearby, and lowered her voice conspiratorially. 'Bit of a looker, isn't he?'

'You go for a bit of blond,' smiled Gwen.

'Shut up,' said Megan. 'Better not let him see that jacket. You keeping it, or what?'

Gwen covered up the security tag in a self-conscious gesture.

'Trina hadn't heard about all this when I phoned her.'

Gwen raised her eyebrows. 'You called Trina before you called me? I could have been trampled to death.'

'You're used to crowd control,' replied Megan offhandedly. It was evident she'd seen nothing of Gwen's activities after she'd raced from the store. 'And Trina's on speed dial. Look at this lot. Bloody students, I told you they were trouble. Rag Week seems to go on for ever, it's just an excuse for them to arse around. All this mad panic for nothing.'

'Someone said they'd been messing with knives.' Robert had sauntered over to join them, and placed his hand on Megan's shoulder. 'People got hurt.' He eyed Gwen thoughtfully. She put her hands behind her back to hide the security tag, and smiled back at him.

'It wasn't students,' said Toshiko Sato, who'd emerged

around the leather goods stall beside them. 'It was skinheads on the rampage. I heard it from the police back there.'

Gwen felt herself relax a little now. 'Megan, this is a friend of mine from work. Tosh, this is—'

'Megan,' beamed Megan. 'I'm one of Gwen's bridesmaids, you know.'

'No, I didn't,' said Toshiko.

Megan was oblivious to her reaction. 'Me and Robert are going to grab a coffee. Laters!' she concluded cheerfully, linked arms with the surprised but pleased shop assistant, and was off. As they went, she glanced over her shoulder and gave Gwen a big grin.

'You tart,' Gwen mouthed at her.

'I know,' Megan mouthed back, wide-eyed.

Toshiko was fiddling about with her PDA now, sweeping it to and fro until she eventually settled on a route to the rear of the mall.

As Gwen retraced her steps to the loading bay, she said to Toshiko: 'They weren't skinheads.'

'Weevils,' agreed Toshiko. 'Yes, you said earlier. But if you seed something like skinheads in people's minds, it's amazing what they think they remember afterwards. I've already dropped some pre-written draft copy in the local press inboxes. Faked a few eyewitness accounts on their participation blogs.'

'What about the CCTV footage?' asked Gwen. They'd reached the circle of transit vans by the loading bays, and she could see the camera rotating on its pole. 'Or is nothing beyond your talents?'

'Certainly not a closed system like that. Nice jacket,' she added. 'Are you going to buy it?'

Gwen smiled, embarrassed, as Toshiko tapped the security

tag on the sleeve. And then gasped when whatever Toshiko did with the PDA harmlessly detached the tag. With barely a pause, Toshiko showed Gwen the display. 'Now look at that – the Rift signature in this area has already died away almost to nothing. That's quick.'

'I haven't seen that sort of alien before, Tosh. Nasty piece of work. Like a bat, but the size of a retriever. And it frightened the crap out of the Weevils.'

'What, literally?'

'It was like…' Gwen pondered the reaction of the cornered Weevil. 'Like they were its prey. I winged it, but it kept coming. We need back-up on this.'

'Not any more.' Toshiko closed her PDA. 'Whatever is was, it's long gone.'

'It was right here less than half an hour ago,' insisted Gwen.

'Long gone in Rift terms.'

Gwen sighed in exasperation. 'So where are the others? Why is it just me whose day off gets ruined? I bet Jack and Ianto's date won't be interrupted, will it?'

'Oh, *that's* what they were talking about,' realised Toshiko. 'I think they were going to Ianto's for a meal. He told Jack he was cooking up something special.'

'Something to eat, but maybe not lunch.'

Toshiko affected to look shocked. Her expression changed when she saw the smile slip off Gwen's face. 'What's the matter?'

'Rhys was going to cook *my* lunch. And I'll be tied up here and miss it *again*!'

'No you won't,' said Toshiko. She picked her way carefully down the ramp and into the mall. 'Show me where the Weevils ended up, and I'll arrange clean-up with Owen. You can get off home.'

'That's not fair on you. Don't you think we're stretching ourselves a bit far? We can cope with an alien here and a monster there. But what if there was a rush on, eh? If the Rift got its skates on. How can five of us cope against the world? Against many, many alien worlds?'

They reached the torn remnants of the two Weevils. The animals remained locked in a ghastly final embrace. Toshiko appraised the nearby CCTV camera with an expert eye. 'Simple enough to erase any actual photographic evidence of the Weevils from their system.'

Gwen looked unsure. 'Need any help?'

'Can you tell the difference between UTP wire and 75 ohm coaxial cables?'

'Obviously not.'

'In that case, I'll struggle on without you. Go.' Toshiko gave her a little wave. 'Nice boots, by the way. Belstaff?'

Back outside in the trampled marketplace, ambulances were drawing up to collect the last victims. 'Skinheads, out of control,' one of the paramedics was saying.

And beyond him, shoppers continued their calm progress towards retail outlets in the streets, unperturbed by recent events as the prosaic reality of life went on.

FOUR

Idelle Gethin stumbled down the bus, apologising as her bags clunked into people's knees. The driver wasn't waiting for her to get seated, the rotten bastard. Like another few seconds would delay him that much. The bus was gathering speed. With both hands full, Idelle had to balance as best she could without treading on the other passengers' feet. She could see a double seat towards the back section. That would have to do. Her bad knees and bulky frame meant that standing all the way to the terminus wasn't an option.

She wished now she'd got on the earlier bus. But the familiar face of a middle-aged woman through the side window had put Idelle off boarding. She didn't know that woman's name, though Idelle sometimes saw her on this route. The woman couldn't help it; she had the unsettling, bulging-eyes stare of hyperthyroidism. Idelle knew that nasty kids on the bus would tease the poor woman – mean calls of 'pretty Polly' – and Idelle wanted to avoid the embarrassment she herself felt when that happened, too nervous to intervene and stop them. Too worried that they'd turn their attention to mocking her for her weight.

Cefn Welch listened to the growl of the Scania's nine-litre engine as it jumped to second and into traffic. There was a clear stretch now before the next stop and, so long as he negotiated the road works carefully, he could make up for earlier delays and get back on schedule. In the rear-view mirror, he caught a glimpse of someone bouncing down the aisle. It was that fat woman who'd struggled to find the right change. Hurry up and find something, love, he thought. Sixty seats and room for twice that many standing, what are you waiting for?

Unlike his mates at the depot, Cefn loved these new articulated buses. He imagined them rippling through the urban jungle of Cardiff like predators, sleek and purposeful. He loved the positions of the controls in the instrument cluster, his commanding view through the huge single-piece windscreen, the throaty roar of the nine-litre engine. And the smell of new upholstery was a definite improvement on the piss-and-dust stink of those old coaches. Gotta move with the times, he'd told Ronald when the old guy was grumbling about all the changes in the DragonLine bus fleet. And with this thought in mind, Cefn smoothly steered the sinuous creature through the traffic lights as the engine kicked into third.

Daniel Pugh lifted his briefcase onto his lap, so that the fat woman could move down the aisle. The rear section of the bendy bus, beyond the concertina joint, was already standing-room only. Daniel pondered whether to offer up his place. Or would that imply he thought she was pregnant? She might take offence. That had happened before. He'd told Sheila about it that time, but his wife had laughed scornfully at him. 'If you're old enough to take early retirement, Dan, then you're probably entitled to a seat on the bus. It's the young kids who should be surrendering their seats. Give them a nudge.' Like those teenagers – no, probably older than that – playing cards across the aisle. Daniel could see that it wasn't a regular pack of diamonds and spades and whatnot, but a much larger format, more like portrait photographs. Each was garishly illustrated with ugly creatures and had complicated annotations. The backs of the cards said 'MonstaQuest', whatever that was.

'A bit old for that kind of thing, aren't you lads?' he joked.

They smiled back in good humour. 'There's a tournament at the mall today,' they said. 'It's not all chess and bridge, y'know.'

Another tall lad sat behind them, the green-and-white scarf marking him out as a student. This lad caught his eye. Daniel gave him a 'what can you do?' smile and looked away out of the window. He saw his own reflection in the dust-streaked glass. Still a full head of white hair, he thought, and drummed his fingers on his briefcase.

Herold Schoonhoven tugged his brown duffel coat closer and tucked the scarf into the neck. He was reading a book on international commerce, because he had a paper due on Monday. Part of his taught post-grad course in Maritime Studies and Transportation. He'd be able to concentrate better at the library, without the bustle of the bus and the noise of the undergrads in the nearby seats playing with their MonstaQuest card set.

Herold usually cycled in to the university library, a ritual he'd adopted during his undergraduate studies in Amsterdam, but he didn't trust the throng of Cardiff's Saturday traffic. So this morning he'd promised his new girlfriend that he'd take more care. Last month, the pretty Indian girl in the Amphora Bar thought he'd somehow guessed her name. Actually he'd been talking about his course, and kicking himself for his inability to make small talk. The confusion and her gentle laughter had done the trick, and he'd been dating Marine Kalhora since the beginning of term. If he got this paper finished in the uni library this morning, they could both get to the cinema this afternoon. The woman on the bench seat next to him jostled his leg and muttered an apology as she struggled clumsily for something in her coat.

Shona Bolton checked her watch. God, it was 10.30 already, she was going to be so late. As if to make the point, her mobile phone was going off, buzzing and vibrating and demanding her attention like some creature trapped in her pocket. She fumbled for it, guiltily aware that she was poking the guy next to her with her elbow.

Shona had been running late from the moment she woke up. Tom had brought her usual cup of coffee, just like her weekday alarm call, and reminded her that she was meeting their daughter Jenny in town. She'd struggled out of the duvet, into the shower, and through her blinding headache. Constantly nagged by Tom that she'd be late, she'd be really late, yes all right, she'd heard him the first twenty bloody times he'd told her. She left in a rush without drying her hair properly.

As she'd staggered down the road to the bus stop, Tom had chased after her. He'd looked like a goon in his fluffy slippers, frantically waving her mobile phone. 'You forgot it again!' he'd told her breathlessly. 'Give her a call. Tell her you're late.' Shona had shoved the phone into her coat pocket and given Tom another earful for nagging her, but mostly because she didn't like to say she hated the damn thing. Tom had bought two phones – one for Shona, and another for her to give Jenny as a birthday present. So she wasn't going to tell him she could barely work out which buttons to press. Not like Jenny, who loved nothing better than to send her mum videos of places she'd been, people she'd met and, on one embarrassing occasion, a boyfriend she'd been… well, never mind that now.

The photo on the mobile's shiny silver fascia flickered at her – Jenny, taken by her dad on the day he'd bought their phones. Trust her daughter to phone and nag her as well. Jenny would be waiting impatiently, and Shona still had to change at the terminus for the connecting service to Pendefig Mall.

It was a video message. Jenny hesitated about whether to put the phone to her ear or look at it in her palm. She pressed a couple of buttons hopefully. The screen got lighter. And lighter. Until it was impossibly, burningly bright. Within the brilliance, a dark shape materialised from nowhere.

Idelle Gethin had given up hope of reaching the spare seat without taking a tumble. She arranged her bags around her feet, and clutched at a standing pole as she tried to remain upright. Beside her, a woman with messy hair was staring at her mobile phone. Idelle thought the brightness was early morning sun at first. Then there was hot, rank breath in her face. A mouthful of savage teeth snapped towards her. Maddened eyes popped wildly beneath a leathery, furrowed brow. The last thing Idelle thought of was the hyperthyroid woman as this nightmare creature tore at her throat.

Herold Schoonhoven was engrossed in an article on transport performance metrics when the commotion began. Someone was trying to push past the fat woman with the pile of bags. A spray of something squirted across the bus. For a second, Herold thought it was a can fizzing open. But it was a gasp of breath and the spurt of arterial blood splashing over his paper. The undergrads in the nearby seat were yelling in horror. Herold reeled back, his mind struggling to process what he saw. Some sort of wild creature had savaged the fat woman, who dropped to the floor with a final gurgling exhalation. But where had it come from, and who would dress a creature like that?

A rush of foul air ran through the bus. The creature lunged forward, its eyes rolling in its dreadful face. It clawed and scraped its way through into the front section of the bus, raking at everything with sharp talons. Passengers shrank back in terror, unable to press themselves far enough against the cold glass of the windows, trapped in their upholstered bucket seats.

Cefn Welch heard the shouts from behind him. Bloody students arsing around again, he thought. They think that raising money for charity gives them a licence to behave how they want. Well, not on his bus. He'd get past this stretch of road works, pull over, and throw them off. The van in the opposite lane was flashing him, so he pressed down the accelerator and the Scania powered into the gap.

So he wasn't expecting the attack. A hot, sour smell assailed him first. Like the sick-and-shit breath of tramps on the night bus. Then a sharp pain in his left arm. Scorching needles raked his shoulder and throat. He caught his breath in surprise, and was more surprised to find he couldn't breathe. He fell against the emergency exit door, his whole body shaking. A hideous, deformed face leered at him.

The van driver was hooting his horn. Cefn snapped his head up, feeling fresh pain in his neck. Through the huge front windscreen, the road works loomed. Cefn wrenched at the wheel, but the Scania was already careering through the barrier and up a mound of earth. The view through the windscreen angled wildly. The bus powered up the mound, twisting to the right like a rearing animal. The engine continued to roar as though Cefn was still pressing down on the accelerator, but he could no longer feel his left leg.

Daniel Pugh tumbled off his bench and pitched into the aisle. The bus corkscrewed onto its side and slammed down onto the roadway with a splintering crash. The side window crazed as it struck the opposite kerb and scraped along with a rending cry of protest that rivalled any of the screaming inside the vehicle. The connecting axle groaned and sheared as the rear carriage of the bus reluctantly twisted to follow the front section, hurling passengers from their seats with dull thuds as they struck hard surfaces.

When the vehicle finally came to a stop, Shona lay dazed against a smashed window. The fat woman was a dead weight across her, and Shona didn't know whose blood was blurring her vision. The engine continued to rev fruitlessly. The hissing sound of escaping air mingled with the weeping of survivors.

Shona still clutched at her phone. The sounds were getting woollier, more distant. She tried to focus on the little screen. She pressed feebly at the phone, but her fingers felt numb against the fiddly little buttons. Panic was setting in – was that Emergency or Redial or Return Call?

The shrieking roar of a maddened, wounded creature filled the bus. Shona stopped being worried about being late for her daughter, and started worrying about whether she was going to die.

FIVE

The washing up mocked Rhys from across the room. A tottering pile of stacked plates and cups leered at him, like a crockery monster that had taken up residence in the sink. If it was a real alien – and God knows, the things Gwen now told him about, he could almost believe it – his fiancée would no doubt finish it off with her Torchwood handgun. Unfortunately, Rhys was the one who'd promised to finish it off, first thing this morning when he'd kissed Gwen goodbye on her way out. His neck prickled with guilty realisation: another broken promise.

He flicked the receiver on the counter to BBC Radio Wales as background noise, and got stuck in. He caught the end of a news report about an attack by vandals in a shopping mall – that would explain the fire alarm at Pendefig, then. Next it was the sort of 'human interest' stuff that drove him bonkers. David Brigstocke made a report about two Plaid members who'd demanded an inquiry into subsidence at the Assembly building. 'Don't dig too deep,' Rhys shouted at the radio. A cub scout group had dressed up in Halloween gear for a charity clean-up of litter-strewn beaches. A woman was suing a tanning salon because she got severe burns after they allowed her to make four visits in one day. Rhys changed channels with soapy fingers once he realised how loudly he was bellowing at the radio. Maybe he'd catch the Harwood's jingle during an ad break. He was singing 'Who can you trust to wash up your plates?' to himself when the front door clicked and he heard Gwen walk in.

She threw her leather jacket across the arm of the sofa. 'Was that you ranting?' she tutted. 'I could hear you out on the landing.'

'That's no way to talk about my singing.'

Gwen gave a good-humoured yell, and waved away his sudsy embrace. Rhys approached her for a kiss, waggling bubbles at her. 'Weren't you supposed to do that first thing? And where's my lunch on the table, eh?' She watched him dry his hands. 'Not the tea towel, use a proper towel!'

'That's your mother's voice,' teased Rhys. He enveloped her in a big hug, snuggling into her neck. 'Mmm. You're wearing your sexy red top. I love you in that. But I love you more out of it…'

She wriggled with delight. 'This is your excuse for not cooking lunch?'

'I'd have done it sooner, love,' Rhys said, 'but the shops were *mental*.'

He felt her stiffen in his embrace. 'I popped out for a few bits and bobs,' he explained warily. 'Oh, there was a classic I overheard. This woman outside Leckworth's said to her friend, "So, she kept his bus pass because he wouldn't be needing it where he's gone," and her mate said, "What, heaven?" And she said, "No, Carmarthen".'

Gwen disengaged herself and folded her arms. 'Leckworth's?'

'And Banana said, "That there, Rhys, is the true voice of Cowbridge Road"…' He faltered under her glare.

'That would be Leckworth's in Pendefig Mall?' Gwen was using her mother's tone of reprimand. Rhys decided not to mention that just at the moment. 'You *promised* me, Rhys.'

'I didn't go near the dress shop.'

'And you took God's gift to Welsh women with you, too! I might have known.'

Rhys made a placating gesture, then grabbed the MonstaQuest cards off the counter. 'Banana wasn't there for long,' he lied. He offered the large deck of cards to her, half apology, half peace offering. 'I got these for him as a joke. Might be good for the day, don't you think?'

She practically snatched them out of his twitching fingers. 'Never mind Banana Boat,' she hissed. 'He'd still be stuck in Lanzarote if Torchwood hadn't pulled some strings with the Spanish.'

Rhys scowled. 'Well, thank you Torchwood, as usual.'

'Who d'you think got him through Arrecife Airport? I should have told Ianto to arrange him a full-cavity search at Customs. See how many DVDs he was smuggling.'

'CDs,' corrected Rhys, and immediately winced with regret.

Gwen flung the MonstaQuest deck at Rhys, skimming it like a Frisbee past his head. It hit the radio, detuning it in the middle of a jaunty ad jingle. The cellophane cover on the card deck split, spilling multicoloured cards over the counter and onto the tiled floor.

'Whoa, whoa, whoa!' Rhys showed her his palms in an effort to calm her. He switched the radio off at the plug, and sighed as he considered a couple of the cards that floated in the tired-looking dishwater. Gwen continued to glower at him. She put a hand to her mouth and broke the gaze. Rhys saw there were tears in her eyes. 'This isn't about Banana, is it?' He took her arm gently, and didn't let her shake him off. 'It isn't about the shopping trip either. What's happened, love?'

'You weren't to know,' she said softly, and went to sit on the sofa. 'I left Tosh to tie up the loose ends. There was an attack at the Pendefig Mall this morning.'

'Oh, well, I left when I heard the fire alarm go off. Radio says it was kids arsing around. I saw one of them. Stupid Halloween mask. Throwing his weight around on the escalators.'

'It wasn't kids.'

'Hooligans, then. Probably rehearsing for the match this afternoon.'

'Not hooligans. It wasn't a mask, Rhys. It was a real, live, deadly dangerous Weevil.'

'I thought it was a teenager,' Rhys mused. 'You told me that Weevils don't like bright places. They prefer gloomy surroundings. Nocturnal. Skulking around with their own kind.' He considered this for a second or two. 'Now that I think about it, that sounds more like teenagers, don't it?'

'Definitely a Weevil,' insisted Gwen.

'Like that thing you showed me in your underground cells?' Rhys gave a low whistle. 'Wow. I didn't look at yours all that closely. But still, you don't expect to see one at the shops.'

'And something else. Something worse.'

Rhys sat next to her, and Gwen let him put his arm around her. 'No trouble for you, I'll bet. Hey,' he went on, 'remember them first few days on the beat? Thought you'd never cope with the yobbos. Now you're more used to handling the

Creature from the Black Lagoon…'

'People died, Rhys,' Gwen persisted. She studied his surprise.

'What?'

'I couldn't stop them.' Gwen heaved a disconsolate little sigh. 'You wouldn't have stopped them. And you could have been killed. Right before our wedding.'

'C'mon,' he cajoled her. 'Is this what our marriage is gonna be like then, Gwen? You can't protect me every day. I'm a big lad now. Maybe a bit too big, but the suit's booked now and I'll just have to fit…'

'You shouldn't underestimate what you don't understand.'

'Thanks,' he grumbled. 'That one of Jack's sayings, is it? "What doesn't kill us just makes us stronger," is that another of his? Or what about "Tomatoes show the difference between knowledge and wisdom"?'

'I have no idea what you're banging on about…' Her voice trailed off, and she stood up.

Bloody hell, Rhys, you've done it now. 'All right, I should have told you,' he admitted. 'I'm sorry.'

Gwen hunkered down in front of him to briefly place her hands on his thighs and kiss him. 'I'm sorry too.' She moved over to the counter. 'And I shouldn't have thrown these…' She was at the sink, picking bedraggled cards out of the dirty water between thumb and forefinger.

Rhys joined her, scooping some of the scattered deck from the tiled floor. The stylishly portrayed creatures snarled and threatened, harmless cartoon monsters. He didn't understand why they were so popular with students and the like. He picked fluff off a couple of them and stacked most of the deck back together. Most of them were still presentable, and if he had to discard the ones that had dropped into the sink, well Banana wouldn't notice or care.

'Where d'you get these?' Gwen asked. She was frowning at one of the cards from the sink. 'Rhys, did you look at these properly?' She showed him the face of one card. It said it was a 'Toothsome'. The cartoon monster's brow was furrowed even more than Gwen's.

'I got them from a games shop in the mall. They had costumes in there, too. So when I saw a yob in a Halloween mask, I didn't give it a second thought…' His voice trailed off as he made the connection for himself. 'Not a yob, you said.'

Gwen shook her head. 'A Weevil. The Cardiff sewers' best-kept secret, thanks to Torchwood.'

Rhys took the damp card from her and looked at it. Suddenly the cartoon creature didn't appear so harmless. 'What's a games shop doing selling cards and Halloween masks of monsters no one knows about?'

Gwen had grabbed her jacket from the sofa, and was already at the short flight of stairs that led out of their apartment. 'Let's go and find out. You're going to show me where that shop is. No matter what the danger, eh?'

Rhys hesitated for a moment. 'What doesn't kill us just makes us stronger?'

'You're a big lad now.' She threw him the car keys. 'I'll let you drive.'

SIX

Snow in November would have suited Amur, thought Malcolm Berkley. The zookeeper watched the magnificent orange-brown Bengal tiger prowl around the limits of her compound as she explored the familiar concrete boundaries with her usual incurious grey-blue stare. She'd been like this for a month, ever since the death of the other tiger, the White Bengal called Ussuri. Tigers tended to be solitary, and until the zoo worked out how to introduce another companion animal, life would be lonelier and colder for Amur in the absence of her snow-white companion.

But there was no prospect of snow today. On this freezing Saturday morning in November, the skies were a solid, icy blue with no clouds in sight, no downpour in prospect.

Torlannau Zoological Park was quiet, so close to opening time, and the staff were preparing for the arrival of visitors. Saturday morning was the day for Amur's treat. Most feeds included heart and ground beef, with a smattering of vitamins and minerals smuggled into the mix. Today there'd be a whole rabbit. Some days, thought the keeper, the animals ate better than he did. Maybe if he was feeling generous he would throw in a cow femur, too. That might enliven the afternoon viewings. The public loved to see the big cat gnawing on a large bone. It made Malcolm laugh to watch the kids in their tiger-print earmuffs as they pressed their eager faces to the plate glass of the transparent wall that separated them from the big cat. That and the brick-and-concrete wall around it in front of the six-metre-wide moat, of course.

Amur continued her circuit of the compound, skirting easily past the twisted trunk of a tree near the centre of the compound. She knew if she touched it, the electrified wires around its base would give her a gentle but discouraging shock. There was no likelihood of her climbing up and launching herself over the moat from its decorative branches.

A flutter of movement in the tree caught Malcolm Berkley's eye. A large carrion crow, perhaps, dropping bravely on a fast raid, taking a chance to forage in the scraps of Amur's last meal.

That was no bird. It was a young man. What the hell was he doing in there? Surely it couldn't be one of the other keepers, he wasn't wearing the blue and yellow Torlannau uniform, nor the white coveralls of the service staff. Berkley choked off a warning cry – unsure whether his shout would cause the man to panic and the tiger to locate him. He reached to his belt for the walkie-talkie, and cursed under his breath when his hand found nothing. He'd left it on his desk back in the administration building. Even in the biting cold of the morning, a colder chill ran through him.

He couldn't leave the man in there. Berkley ran at full pelt around the enclosure, skittering on the gravel pathway, hurrying to the keeper's entry for the enclosure. He had his security keycard, thank God. Berkley fumbled it into the access mechanism, and slipped softly through. He swiftly negotiated the outer gates, and snatched up a bucket of ready-prepared ground beef. He might need that to distract the big cat and get the man out to safety.

The inner door creaked on its unoiled hinge, a hideously penetrating noise in this freezing air. Amur's head twisted round; she recognised the sound.

'Get over here!' snapped Berkley to the intruder.

The intruder turned to face him. Berkley felt his own cold fear turn to hot anger. It was Gareth!

'Gareth, what the hell are you doing? Walk over here now! Don't dawdle, but don't run. You must remember the drill?'

Gareth just stood and smiled. He was three or four years older than Berkley remembered. Longer hair, shabbier appearance. But still recognisably the summer student who'd worked at Torlannau.

'Mr Berkley.' Gareth's laconic, mocking words showed a disturbing lack of concern.

'Are you on drugs?' hissed Berkley.

Gareth waved his mobile phone at Berkley. It looked like an ugly, clunky, old-fashioned model.

Berkley stared. 'You'll get yourself killed. Maybe both of us! That tiger hasn't been fed today…'

'What tiger?' Gareth put his hand to his forehead and peered around him, for all the world like an old-fashioned sailor looking out to sea.

Berkley checked to see where Amur was. Not in sight. Not behind the narrow bole of the single tree. He whipped his head from side to side, disbelieving. No sign of the big striped cat. Could she have slipped down into the moat? That would only allow her access via a ramped tunnel on the far side and back into the main exhibit area. Amur wouldn't try to leap the moat because on the far side of it there was only the ninety-degree vertical of smooth concrete and glass that Berkley checked daily for defects.

No, that couldn't be right. He could see straight across into the visitor area of the zoo. The smooth wall had simply vanished. The tiger *could* have leaped that gap.

The trespasser walked across to the zookeeper. That thing in his hand wasn't a mobile phone. The shape was too irregular, the flashing lights too bizarre.

'What's going on, Gareth?'

The young man made a flicking gesture at him. A flat piece of card spun from Gareth's fingers, and the zookeeper flinched involuntarily. It looked like a photograph of some kind, maybe one of the big postcards they sold in the zoo shop. Berkley grew angry. He stooped to pick the card up from the sandy ground, and saw it wasn't a photo but a line drawing of a monstrous creature, accompanied by some sort of numerical assessment.

Berkley considered the intruder with contempt. 'Stop playing games, Gareth. You were bugger all use when you were on work experience, but surely you remember the rules about the large cats?'

'Solitary animals,' Gareth smiled. 'They don't run with the pack. I like that about them.'

'This isn't funny, Gareth.'

'But you like a joke, don't you, Mr Berkley?' sneered Gareth. 'Do you remember how I learned about the big cats? How you thought it was such fun to let me through the outer gate and then lock me in. Before I knew there was an inner safety gate, of course. You let me crap myself with fear. I literally crapped myself. Did you know that, Mr Berkley? Did you?'

The man had lost his mind, thought Berkley. No matter

what gags the zoo staff played on the students, that couldn't explain, wouldn't excuse, this. He eyed the insane gap in the far enclosure wall. His mind reeled as he considered the priorities. Alert the other zoo staff. Work his way to one of the tranquilliser guns stashed in one of five secure locations around the park. But first, get this crazy guy to safety.

'All right, lad.' Berkley stood, and held out an encouraging hand. 'Let's get you of here.'

Gareth wasn't listening. He pointed to the card that Berkley now held. 'Reckon you can handle big animals, do you, Mr Berkley?'

Berkley brushed sand off the card illustration. It had a colourful motif on the reverse: MonstaQuest. The face revealed a stylised cartoon. A two-headed dragon leered at him, both sets of slavering jaws filled with an improbable number of needle-sharp teeth.

Gareth stood close to him now, and handed over another of the MonstaQuest cards. The new one represented a storm, angled blue lines marking out the falling rain. Barely had Berkley registered this than he felt the patter of water on his head and shoulders. Within seconds, it was like someone had turned a hose on him. The sky above remained a cloudless icy blue, but all around his feet the ground was darkening and the sand was thickening into slurry.

The slam of the compound gate told him that Gareth had left. Berkley heard the bolt draw across. With a yell, he staggered over to the exit. The gate was secure and locked. Gareth was nowhere to be seen.

Berkley moved back into the enclosure. Beyond where the missing wall should have been, he could make out that the rest of the park was still dry. But there was no way to get across the moat.

61

And how could it be raining solely in the tiger compound?

Now there was another sound. A shrieking cacophony of bestial noise like he'd never heard in his twenty years at the zoo. A scaly pointed tail flicked into his side, winding him and throwing him to the hard ground. Berkley rolled onto his back, smearing sand and grit on his cheeks as he swiped at the rain that streamed down his face.

A creature leered down at him. It was the impossible double-headed dragon from the MonstaQuest card. Both its heads bellowed and slavered in uncontained rage, as though fighting between themselves for priority.

The monster stood between him and the locked exit gate. The moat was impossible to clear. Berkley scrambled over to the tree in the centre of the compound, but the wires around the base jolted him with a painful electric shock.

Malcolm Berkley lay panting in the mud and the rain. He managed to close his eyes and scream just before the nightmare creature decided which of its jaws would strike first.

SEVEN

Toshiko wasn't impressed with Lloyd Maddock. The prematurely balding general manager of the Pendefig Mall had been sneeringly dismissive when she first approached him. He had flip-flopped completely once she'd flashed her winning smile and reminded him of the appointment she'd sneaked into his online calendar. An unscheduled review of security by the Pendefig parent company. So it was a bit rich now for him to be telling her, in his plummy, pause-filled Swansea accent, that his *brilliant* team always worked *so hard* to give customers the best shopping experience in Wales, when his 'specially trained Customer Services team' were busy bundling his customers off-site as the fire alarm clamoured and echoed around them.

Toshiko told him she wanted to see the CCTV tapes. Maddock wasn't able to raise the security coordinator on his radio. The landlines seemed to have packed in, too. 'Must have been knocked out by that blast of wind that blew through the whole place,' suggested Maddock. 'Just wait till I see those contractors. Recommended by Head Office, they were. But they must have completely screwed up the air conditioning.' There was an embarrassed pause while he evidently remembered that Toshiko was from the Head Office whose judgement he had just questioned. In the awkward silence, Maddock surveyed the pit of the mall as the escalator took them higher. 'Ambulances, police... God knows if the insurance will cover this.' This thought made him brighten visibly. 'Maybe an Act of God means the mall won't be liable?'

Toshiko did not share his callous enthusiasm. She scowled back at the general manager. 'Why don't we go and find Mr Belden in the security suite?' Toshiko bit her lip. It wouldn't do to let Maddock know just how much she already knew about the layout or staffing of Pendefig. She slipped the tell-tale PDA into her jacket pocket, and showed her smile again.

Maddock rubbed his hands together with invisible soap, and unctuously agreed to chaperone her to his 'state-of-the-art security facility' on the upper level. Toshiko had to endure a lecture on the mall's dedication to quality, choice of retailers, and exciting mall promotions. She doubted whether anything as exciting as a Weevil attack had happened in Pendefig before.

A thin sheen of sweat formed a patina on Maddock's high pale forehead. He wiped at it with the back of his hand, then wiped his hand on the tails of his jacket.

'Nice suit,' observed Toshiko.

'Jasper Littman,' grinned Maddock. 'Bespoke.'

That suit wasn't bought in Pendefig Mall, thought Toshiko. No matter how much he banged on about the ten-million-pound refurbishment, Maddock thought he was way too good for this place. His enthusiasm was as synthetic as these plants that filled the gap between the up and down escalators.

She asked him: 'Why are these flowers all fake?'

'They don't need watering,' replied Maddock. 'Dusting occasionally. There's no natural light in the mall.'

'Why not?' Even the Hub had some outside light artfully reflected into its underground location, thought Toshiko. 'Is it like casinos? So that people forget how long they've been in here? Keep spending.' She looked around them. 'No clocks either.'

Maddock responded with a thin smile, and began a long explanation about how it was a contemporary design feature to upgrade the principal trading areas beneath unglazed roofing. Toshiko sensed her eyes were glazing over instead.

They reached the top of the upper escalator that led to the highest level. To their left, a U-shaped staircase led up to the security suite. No escalator for the staff, Toshiko noted. Open-tread steps, scratched wooden handrail.

No shops on this level yet either. Just a handful of boarded-up units waiting for the retail recovery that might make it attractive to rent this far up in the mall. A library filled the whole opposite side of the open square. Behind a wide stretch of plate-glass windows, vivid posters advertised books, DVDs, readings and Halloween events.

Except that one of the splashes of bright colour wasn't a poster. It was a wide smear of blood, smudged upwards until it reached head height. Toshiko scanned the residue, blue lights flickering over the cracked glass. 'Human,' she said to herself. A red trail dribbled away towards the emergency stairs, suggesting a creature with four splayed toes and with a rear claw on the foot. There appeared to be two sets of scuffed, bloody tracks – one towards the stairs and the other back from it. They were distinct, not overlapping, so Toshiko couldn't tell which was fresher. Whether the creature would be waiting for her in the stairwell or whether it had already left. Her PDS revealed no residual Rift energy signs.

'Wait there,' she called to Maddock.

Maddock had only just seen the trail of blood. He covered his mouth with both hands. When he looked up at Toshiko, there was a wild look of horror in his eyes. 'The police…' he eventually mumbled.

'On their way,' she lied. The police would be on their way only when she called them in, and that wouldn't be until she'd assessed the area. 'Wait there,' she reiterated. She slammed the emergency stop, and the escalator snapped off with a mechanical sigh. 'If anyone comes up that, send them straight back down again. Can you do that?'

He stared at her, uncertain.

'Can you do that?' she persisted.

Maddock nodded dumbly. He fiddled with his mobile phone.

'Don't make any calls,' Toshiko told him. She deliberated on another plausible lie. Didn't want him calling in the police, or his mates, before she'd swiftly recce-ed the whole area. 'Need to keep those lines clear for the emergency services.'

Maddock complied meekly. He plunged his shaking hands in his expensive jacket pockets and gazed with expectant, frightened eyes down the escalator and into the depths of the mall.

Toshiko slipped into the emergency stairwell and cautiously followed the trail of blood.

She found the body on the next landing down. From what was left, Toshiko worked out it was a woman in her twenties. The body was twisted, limbs thrown out awkwardly amid crumpled plastic shopping bags. The upper torso was a shredded mess of ripped clothing and torn flesh. A savage slash across the neck had severed her carotid artery, and the wound had spurted lines of dark red blood up against the chipped grey concrete of the wall. The body was cooling. Toshiko closed the corpse's appalled, staring eyes.

A scratchy electronic noise came from a lower stair. Toshiko found the open clamshell of a silver mobile phone. She picked it up and listened to a chaotic chatter. 'Hello, who's there?' she asked.

'Tosh! Tosh, is that you?' the phone said.

She could hardly believe it. 'Owen! Did you call this number, or did she call you?'

'Just found this phone,' Owen's voice continued. He seemed to be talking to someone else nearby as well. 'Having a bit of a busy day here, Tosh.'

'Where are you?'

'I'm just in—' The line abruptly clicked off.

'OK,' Toshiko said to dead air. She was about to click the phone shut when the speaker crackled and a mechanical voice said: 'Achenbrite apologise for the interruption in service. Please stand by.' The message repeated. Toshiko pocketed the mobile, and tapped the connector point by her right ear that activated her Torchwood comms. The same message was repeating: 'Achenbrite apologise...' She tapped it off again.

That couldn't happen. The Torchwood system was a dedicated network. The screen of her PDA flickered with interference patterns, too. Maybe she could check with Ianto, he might have some idea what—

She realised she'd instinctively tapped her earpiece again. Easy to get into that habit. Easy to get over-reliant on the technology, she of all people should know that.

Back up by the library, she found Maddock frowning at his

mobile phone. She could hear the same message playing out of it. 'Thought I told you not to use that thing,' she rebuked him, and made for the U-shaped stairway. 'I'm going to make that CCTV check now. You said it was Mr Belden in charge?' He hadn't; her PDA had told her that earlier, but the question helped focus the frightened general manager.

The U-shaped stairs up to the security suite revealed further clues. Close up, the handrail wasn't just scratched, it was raked along most of its length. Toshiko considered the angle of the freshly gouged grooves and the spatter-pattern of blood on the wall. So the creature had come down this way, leaned against the library window on the lower level, and found an exit in the emergency stairwell. Some unfortunate shopper had bumped into it there and got torn to pieces. The creature had made its way across the upper floor, and then back up these stairs. Toshiko gripped the butt of her handgun, and guardedly negotiated the remaining stairs to the top-most floor.

The door of the security room had been wrenched out of place. A chunk of plaster beside the hinges was missing. The cracked door lay on the floor. A severed human arm, still incongruously clad in the pale blue sleeve of a mall uniform, stretched across it at an angle, its stiff fingers never to reach the handle.

The PDA screen continued to fizz unhelpfully. No way of telling if there was recent Rift activity up here. No way of tracing the creature.

The door would have opened inwards, but the lintel had splintered out into the corridor, shards of wood spiking in Toshiko's direction as she approached. Whatever had smashed down the door had done so from within the security room.

And inside was a slaughterhouse.

Toshiko had attended murder scenes, and been in abattoirs, yet this made her stomach heave. She knew from the records that the place was designed for two people; it was still hard at first glance to count the bodies. Shreds of pinkish flesh and pale blue cloth were strewn over the floor, chairs, and equipment. A deep slick of blood pooled on the carpet tiles, so much that a raised patch had congealed. What equipment had not been smashed flickered and clicked, unobserved by the butchered guards.

Toshiko tried to concentrate on something else, to stay calm. She studied the multiplexor that showed quad images – a trade-off between getting greater coverage versus the complexity of post-editing. That looked like a matrix switcher. The images on this monitor here were lo-def colour, but those were black and white. Better for low light. An IR camera covered the loading dock, where she and Gwen had encountered the Weevils earlier. It used a motion detector, so that it could record frames of video only when there was movement and thus reduce the subsequent need to review large chunks of nothing.

But her eyes were inevitably drawn to the ravaged bodies of the dead men in the room. One of them lay half-covered by some odd foliage that was growing in the corner. Variegated leaves with a serrated edge. Not a good place to keep plants, she thought. Anything that needs watering shouldn't be that close to expensive electrical equipment.

A rattle made her spin abruptly. Her heart hammered, and her breath caught in her throat. Her handgun was level and ready, aimed at the doorframe.

'There's someone up on the roof,' said Maddock. He broke off as he saw her gun. And then he saw the carnage in the room. 'Oh God,' he managed before his eyes rolled back in his head and he tumbled back into the corridor.

Toshiko stepped carefully over to him. Maddock was unconscious, but apparently unharmed. She put him in the recovery position. At least she wouldn't have to explain to him why Head Office staff were armed these days.

A scratching noise came from the flight of nearby stairs that led up to the roof. Fresh blood trailed up the concrete steps.

Her PDA was still out of action. No way of telling what was up there. It could be the creature that had butchered the security guards, or it could be one of its would-be victims who'd escaped. She needed to find out.

Toshiko angled her gun up the short stairwell and kept close to the outer wall. The handrail and the concrete paint were smeared red where something had hurried up ahead of her, but this was no time to be fastidious about getting in on her clothes. She remembered Jack warning her about this during basic training: 'Better red than dead,' he'd joked. Except that staying alive wasn't a joke. Her dry cleaner had seen worse than this and not asked any questions. But then again, her dry cleaner was Ianto.

She pushed at the crash bar and the fire door swung open with a squeal of unoiled hinges. She moved swiftly through the frame and out, and pressed her back against the adjacent wall. She narrowed her eyes until they adjusted to the sudden brightness.

The roof was laid out as a series of metal walkways. The blockish square shapes of air conditioning vents and lift mechanisms stood out starkly against the clear morning sky. A light wind carried the sounds of traffic and industry up to her. Cardiff sparkled off into the distance on three sides of the roof.

And a dark silhouette stared down over the edge.

The creature was the size of a large dog. It squatted like a dark gargoyle at the far edge of the roof, facing away from her. Its tall pointed ears swivelled, scanning ahead. What at first appeared to be a broad humped back was actually a pair of folded wings. They flexed as though the thing was about to fly off the roof. The head moved side-to-side, like a cat judging the position of its prey.

With no connection on her PDA, Toshiko tried to remember the layout of the building she'd seen earlier. Maybe the images were still in the PDA's memory, but there was probably only time to rely on her own. This side of the mall overlooked the multi-storey car park. So, the creature was sizing up people as they parked their vehicles.

The wings unfurled. Thin layers of veined black skin stretched over a frame of thin bones, with a small tear in one wing. Short clawed hands flexed at the ends, long talons visible against the sky. It was like an enormous predatory bat.

A bat the size of a retriever. Wasn't that what Gwen had seen?

And it was preparing to fly.

Toshiko squared her feet, bracing herself to fire. The walkway beneath her clanked as the metal moved. At the sound, the dark creature immediately twisted to face her. Beneath those tall ears was a small, savage face, half-filled by a mouth that bristled with razor-sharp, foam-flecked teeth. It quickly repositioned its legs, swirled its wings into position, and prepared to launch itself at her.

She squirted off a couple of panicky shots. One flew wide, but the other tore through the leathery membrane of skin in the creature's right wing. It howled a scream of rage, and sprang towards her.

Toshiko dropped to one side, rolling off the metal walkway. The gravel-covered surface of the roof sagged under her weight, and she struggled to recover her position.

The bat-creature was on her with frightening speed. Toshiko's head thumped against metal. Lights sparkled dizzily, and a nauseous wave threatened to engulf her. Claws raked her jacket. She threw one arm over her face as she tried to get the other, gun-hand between herself and her attacker. But the creature smacked out dismissively with one of its rear feet, and the gun clattered away into the distance and over the edge of the roof.

The edges of Toshiko's vision clouded into darkness.

The monster pressed its weight on her chest. The tiny, savage head pushed close to hers, its mouth wide, its scream filling her ears.

Toshiko thought of the torn remains in the security room, and wondered what would be left of her to identify the body.

There was a hard push on her torso. The creature jumped off her and towards the edge of the roof.

Toshiko hadn't even noticed that she had forgotten to breathe. She started to suck in air again, greedily, desperately. Why had the creature stopped? She wanted to look where the thing had gone, but her body felt too heavy to move, and her eyes just wanted to close.

A static crackle hissed in the air nearby. The bat-creature howled again, though the sound seemed to fade and die in the air. Toshiko forced herself to look. Two men in grey boiler suits were stalking across the roof. Were those rifles they carried? They had shoulder-stocks and scopes, and the men carried them like weapons; but the barrel fanned out into a bulbous end, incongruously like a garden hose. These devices spat out a cloudy spray that fizzed and coiled towards the cowering creature.

The two men stepped past Toshiko, ignoring her. She tried to call out, but her voice failed. They couldn't have missed her; they were simply ignoring her.

The bat-like creature was a long way off now. It must be a hundred metres away.

But that wasn't possible, because the roof wasn't that wide. The bat-like monster was shrinking, diminishing, struggling within the fizzing cloud of particles sprayed from the rifles. One of the men produced a small container, no bigger than a shoebox. He tugged on a pair of thick gloves before he scooped the helpless creature into the box.

Toshiko felt unconsciousness overwhelming her. The last thing she noticed before she closed her eyes was the insignia on the men's boiler suits. A stylised device of crossed keys, and a single word: Achenbrite.

EIGHT

The Withington Hotel was not infested with alien bedbugs. Which wasn't to say that it didn't have unpleasant biting insect life in its five-star bedrooms, reflected Owen Harper.

Jack had asked him to pursue this investigation. 'A safe pair of hands,' Jack had called him. Yeah, right. What Jack meant was that it would be a safe assignment for him in his condition. Nothing would get broken, particularly Owen.

Dead Man Walking. What was the point in coming back to life if Torchwood wouldn't find him any death-defying assignments?

One of Toshiko's monitoring software programs had identified an unexpected peak in GP records about urticaria, with a statistically significant increase in patients with red, itchy weals on their skin. Cross-checking credit card details suggested a further statistically significant link to the Withington Hotel, a Rift hotspot some three months previously.

At least Jack now allowed Owen to carry his handgun again. 'Not that it'll be much good for picking off alien insects,' Ianto had explained when he'd delivered the weapon from the Armoury that morning. 'You're not that good a shot.'

'Well, how could I defend myself again alien bedbugs?' pondered Owen.

'Tuck your trousers into your socks,' Ianto had suggested, with no indication that he was joking.

Owen arrived at the Withington shortly before 10 a.m. and spent less than an hour masquerading as a hotel inspector. Enough time to send the hotel management into a minor panic, and also sufficient for Owen to access all necessary areas. He swiftly identified the reason for so many bitten guests as *cimex lectularis* – the common bedbug. Even the honeymoon suite had evidence of eggs, faecal spots, and a lively collection of first-instar nymphs.

So, the outbreak had not come through the Rift. However, Owen had identified a missing Vredosian who was working as a chambermaid on the fifth floor. The plaid polyester of the staff uniform anonymised the staff of most large hotels, and yet Owen found it hard to understand how she'd gone unrecognised with her triangular teeth and pale grey skin. Hedgehog spines poked through her mop cap, like Mrs Tiggy-Winkle. He studied his captive as they both waited for the lift to arrive. 'How did no one notice you?'

The Vredosian wriggled uncomfortably beside him, her thumbs cuffed together. 'The staff captain thought I was from Eastern Europe,' she rasped. 'Sometimes the obvious stares him in the face.'

Owen laughed. 'I've got a Captain like that.'

The lift pinged. He was about to give the Vredosian an encouraging push into the lift when he remembered that she was the source of the bedbug outbreak. He wasn't sure he wanted to get that close to her in the lift, but what was the alternative? He needed to get her back to the Hub. And then what – a bowl of bread and milk? He supposed Jack would know. 'So, you've travelled millions of miles to find the job of your dreams,' he said, and indicated she should board the lift. 'Working for the minimum wage in a South Wales Hotel. Doesn't get better than that, eh?'

The Vredosian lowered her spiny eyelashes and ignored him. She wasn't dangerous; just another bloody nuisance in a city that already had enough of them to worry about without a flea-carrying extraterrestrial working illegally in the Welsh service industry. God, just imagine the *Daily Mail* headline.

Owen studied his own reflection in the mirrored wall of the lift. Is this what he'd become – a nursemaid to vagrant aliens? He put his left hand up to his face experimentally, aware again that he could feel nothing. The glove covered his permanently broken left finger. It also enclosed the tatty crepe bandage that held the splint in place, in turn concealing the scalpel cut across his palm that would never heal and that required re-stitching each week. He stroked one finger down a sideburn. The first day home after his return from the dead, he'd had a careful shave – his final shave, as it happened. He'd never have five o'clock shadow again. The beard would never grow back. On the bright side, he'd never get hair in his ears like his dad. And he'd had to decide, right then in front of the bathroom mirror in his apartment, whether he wanted to lose those sideburns for the rest of his life. No, not life – his *existence*.

Owen was still contemplating this when the lift pinged for the ground floor, the mirrored doors slid open, and his reflection disappeared.

The pair stepped into the lobby area. Bright morning sunshine spilled through the revolving doors and sparkled on the brass fittings. Orange pumpkin decorations glowed as though they had internal illumination. A couple of kids bounced on the leather couches while their parents waited in the check-out line.

Should have taken the service lift to the basement, thought Owen. He had to get the Vredosian across town to the Hub. What was he gonna do, order a taxi? He hadn't brought his car, but he was damned if he was going to call Ianto to get assistance. And Toshiko would be so solicitous, so eager, so nice about everything that he didn't think he could bear it.

He didn't have to think about it for long. From beyond the revolving door came the sound of car horns, angry shouting, and a tremendous crash of metal and glass. There was a flurry of movement in the lobby as guests and staff hurried to look out of the windows. From the first shocked comments he overheard, Owen knew there'd been a serious traffic accident.

Quite how serious he didn't know until he and the Vredosian got out into the street. The sound of pedestrians screaming was brutally loud once he'd got through the revolving door. Further along the street one of those jointed single-deck buses lay cracked and helpless, partly embedded in a glass shopfront. The DragonLine bus had evidently mounted the angled earthworks by the road repairs, twisting as it went, and then slid helplessly along the road until it mounted the opposite pavement. The concertinaed front of a white van showed where it had careered into oncoming traffic before finally coming to rest with its roof jammed into Wendleby's department store. Jagged panes from what remained of the store's plate-glass window rained down like murderous icicles. The rear of a big display poster flapped into the street. He could just read the remains of the shredded banner: 'MonstaQuest Demonstration Today!' it declared.

Owen fully expected that he was the first medic on the scene. Beside him in the shadow of the Withington Hotel's Edwardian portico, the Vredosian flicked surreptitious glances to either side, judging whether she could make a break for freedom. Owen considered the yells of the pedestrians and the roar of the felled bus's engine. He tutted at the Vredosian and tossed over the key to the thumb-cuffs. 'Your lucky day,' he told her. He jogged over to the crash scene, muttering: 'Some of these won't have been so fortunate.'

He pushed past the early rubberneckers. 'Stay back,' he snapped at them. A peroxide blonde gave him a surly look. 'You got a mobile?' he asked her

'Yeah,' she said.

Owen stared straight at her. 'Phone 999.' The blonde looked surprised. 'Do it now,' he told her. She was so shocked that she did so straight away.

The filthy underside of the bus growled angrily nearby, mud and water dripping from its grimy surfaces. The engine was still churning and the transmission whirled. Owen ran round to the back of the bus and slammed his glove on the emergency stop. The engine chattered into silence, which made the hiss of leaking air and the screams of the passengers more audible.

A black and white cab was squished up onto the pavement between Wendleby's and the overturned rear section of the bus. Owen jumped on the bonnet, then over its cracked 'For Hire' sign and up onto the side of the bus. He traversed the length of the coachwork, sensing the metal panels give beneath his weight as he approached the front. The DragonLine emblem, a stylised motif in red and green, twisted its way down the painted body, as though marking out a path for him. At the snarling head of the painted dragon, the orange lights of the destination board in its jaws flashed intermittently, unable to decide where the bus was headed; 207 Lisvane via Llanishen stuttered into 102 Victoria Park and back again.

There was a banging sound from beneath his feet. Owen looked down and saw a scared face looking up at him in desperation. A middle-aged woman hammered with a bloodied fist against the entry doors, slamming against strips of glass that had now become the ceiling that trapped her inside the bus. She forced her fingers through the rubber seal, desperate to pry the doors apart. The blood on her fingers made it too slick to grasp, and her fingers slipped out of sight. She smacked against the glass in utter frustration, leaving a smeared bloody palm print on the glass.

Owen waved her away, hit the emergency door control, and kicked hard on the doors. They flick-flacked open, and he dropped carefully through the gap.

The bus was filled with terrified shouts and screams. The noise worried Owen most. Since he'd lost his senses of touch and taste and smell, he'd become more attuned to sights and sounds. With one side of the vehicle pressed against the pavement, half of the windows were now obscured which meant the flickering lights cast a twilight pall over the interior.

An angry man in his twenties tried to seize Owen's lapels, but Owen eased him aside. 'I'm a doctor,' he said loudly but calmly. 'Let me help these people. You seem to be mobile?'

The angry man looked a little cowed.

'Good,' continued Owen briskly. 'So help these people climb out of the front doors. I'll check on the others.'

In the crash, passengers on the left had been thrown forward and to the right. People struggled to free themselves from the piled bodies crushed against the roadside windows. As the walking wounded struggled forward to the newly opened doors, Owen decided to start his triage at the back of the vehicle. He stepped gingerly on the edges of seats, making his way to the rear, calling for calm. Bodies slumped against windows that were etched in red where blood had seeped through the cracked glass. And beyond that, the stark grey of the road. Hands grasped at his legs as he passed. He muttered apologies for not stopping, and promised to return.

Owen reached the rear of the bus at last, and started to offer advice about raising injured limbs and applying pressure to wounds. He knew he himself would be unable to detect pulses, so he directed willing passengers to assist, indicating where they should feel for the carotid or radial arteries.

A woman who might have been in her forties was crying softly, saying over and over that she couldn't stay, her daughter would be waiting, she needed her mobile phone.

'What's your name, my love?' Owen asked her.

'Shona,' said the woman. 'I'm going to be late for my daughter.'

She was wedged in among the bent steel of a seat. She stared up at Owen, her hands clutching the mangled metal frame. As Shona tried to lever herself out, her eyes pleaded with him.

'Give me a hand,' demanded a grey-haired man, nudging Owen's arm.

'It doesn't hurt, Daniel,' said Shona. 'It's just, I'm stuck.'

'We only just met,' said the grey-haired guy. 'Bloody funny time to make new acquaintances. Anyway, barely a scratch on her. Let's get her out of here.'

Owen tugged him aside and spoke directly into the man's ear. 'Can't tell whether she has internal injuries. Please wait.' He looked beneath the seat as the old guy fumed beside him and Shona continued to whimper. Owen could see her legs were twisted out of shape. Fresh blood streamed down. In the cramped and chaotic conditions, he knew he could do nothing for her. She couldn't feel any pain. Owen felt the familiar sick helplessness of his early days in A&E, when he'd been at the site of his first RTA. He wanted to save this woman, get her to her daughter. But he knew it was just a matter of time before she died. He knew what awaited her then. And there was nothing he could do about that, either.

A look passed between him and the old guy. He'd seen the blood now, too. The slightest motion of Owen's head informed the other man. Daniel's eyes started to fill with tears. 'I'll stay with her,' he told Owen. 'Until…' He swallowed the rest of the sentence. 'Until the ambulance men arrive,' he said to Shona, and smoothed the hair from her eyes with a liver-spotted hand. 'Don't you worry about a thing.' He turned aside to Owen and hissed: 'What happened to the brute who started all this? Where is that scumbag?'

Owen's face showed his bafflement.

Daniel was struggling to stay calm for Shona's sake. He jerked his head towards the body of a large woman that was spread-eagled across two broken seats. 'Took a knife to her and then ran off down the bus…' The rest of Daniel's muttered diatribe was lost on Owen, who was studying the tear marks around the fat woman's neck. That ragged edge wasn't like a knife wound. Could she have sustained it in the crash?

A young lad in a university scarf, green and red and white, struggled noisily with the rear emergency door. No, that red was more blood on a Cardiff scarf, wasn't it? The door sprang open, and he started to help people over and out.

Owen gave a hand to a couple of shocked teenage boys. One of their friends was scraping around in the debris and trying to pick things up off the broken seats. 'Leave them, Alwyn!' called one of his mates.

'They're ultra-rare!' bleated Alwyn. 'I can't leave my MonstaQuest cards in all this!'

Owen eased him away by the elbow. 'Even so, it's more important that you leave.' He plucked a couple of the cards out of Alwyn's fingers to make his point, and scrunched them into his own jacket pocket. The lad grumbled, but allowed himself to be hauled to safety by the other teenagers.

Owen rolled his eyes in despair, and looked at where the rest of Alwyn's cards had dropped against the cracked window. In the middle of the scattered pile was a mobile phone, open and flashing. He stretched across and retrieved it, picking bits of glass from the silver fascia. The photo display showed a smiling young woman, labelled 'Jenny'. He could hear a voice on the line. 'Hello, who's there?' it asked.

Bloody hell, thought Owen what are the odds? 'Tosh! Tosh, is that you?'

She sounded just as surprised. 'Owen! Did you call this number, or did she call you?'

She? That would be Jenny. 'Just found this phone,' he explained.

'Is it Jenny?' Shona asked weakly from beside him.

'No, it's someone I know,' he said gently. And then into the phone again: 'Having a bit of a busy day here, Tosh.'

'Where are you?'

'I'm just in the middle of an RTA, outside the…' He trailed off as the sounds of a dead line filled his ear. The call had been interrupted, and there was no connection. Time enough later to call Toshiko back.

Most of the walking wounded had evacuated. Those who remained were the trapped and the dead. A thin voice called from the length of the bus: 'Please help me!'

A middle-aged Chinese guy was bent over a woman. Her long, light-brown hair spilled over the cheap upholstery of a ripped-out seat. Her eyes stared sightlessly. Owen held the man's shoulders and gently pulled him away. He saw that the Chinese guy's right foot was cocked unnaturally over to the left, with a gash through his faded jeans. A serious leg injury could be fatal, and if the femoral artery in the man's thigh was compromised then he might bleed to death within the next ten minutes. Owen clumsily removed the guy's belt and looped it around the injured leg. 'God, what happened here?'

The Chinese guy grimaced as the tourniquet bit. 'Some kid in a Halloween mask went berserk with a knife. Killed the driver. The bus ran out of control.' He gritted his teeth, and his eyes showed his fear. 'Is it a terrorist attack?'

'A knife?' Owen checked the driver, dead in his cab. The man's arm, shoulder and throat were all torn to shreds. Again, not the clean edges from a knife, or from metal and glass laceration.

The Chinese guy lashed out awkwardly with his good leg. His foot connected with a leather-clad figure that had fallen into the seat beside him. The figure stirred and groaned.

'Hey hey hey!' shouted Owen. 'Knock it off!'

'He's the terrorist,' spat the Chinese guy.

That's no terrorist, realised Owen as the figure reared up. It's a Weevil. And it's really badly pissed off.

The Weevil threw back its head and howled. The Chinese

84

guy shrank back, but had nowhere to go. The Weevil's scored face hissed and spat at him.

Owen slapped the Weevil in the face. 'Come and have a go,' he said, 'if you think you're hard enough.'

Christ, he thought as the creature snapped its head round to face him, you'd better be right about this, Harper. Since his resurrection, Owen had discovered that his very presence seemed to cow the creatures into submission. But did this one know he was King of the Weevils? Or was he about to become Snack of the Weevils?

The creature's sunken eyes glittered at him. It growled softly, and lowered its head.

Owen blinked slowly. 'Good boy.'

A brace of emergency vehicles screeched up outside the bus. The area was abruptly bathed in their strobing blue lights, and the bus echoed with the piercing wail of their sirens. Spooked, the Weevil leaped from cover and fled through the bus doors.

Owen struggled around to find his gun in the back of his belt. With so little feeling in his hands, he had to double-check anything that he reached for when it was out of sight. He cursed. Couldn't feel for a pulse, couldn't feel for a gun, what bloody good was he?

By the time he'd scrambled after the Weevil, it had already battered its way past the crowds gathered outside. He watched helplessly as it vanished into a side alley. By the time he got down, the creature would be back in its sewer home eating shitcakes.

Owen slammed the side of the bus in frustration, and got a satisfying clang with the butt of his gun. He registered the shock on the paramedics' faces, and reholstered it. He sat heavily on the side of the overturned bus and swore again.

A flapping shape in Wendleby's window behind him caught his attention, fitfully illuminated by the flashes from the emergency vehicles. If his heart had still been beating, it would have leaped into his mouth. The shape was just the MonstaQuest display poster. But the big cartoon artwork on the poster bore an alarming resemblance to the Weevil.

Owen reached into his jacket pocket and retrieved the couple of crumpled MonstaQuest cards he'd snatched from Alwyn. From each of the oversized playing cards, stylised pictures of Weevils leered back at Owen. Just like the one who'd escaped down the alleyway. They seemed to mock him. King of the Weevils, indeed.

The orange indicator board in the dragon's jaws seemed to have decided its status at last: 'Out of Service'. That reminded him about his interrupted call with Toshiko. He tapped near his earlobe, and called in to speak to her.

What the hell…?

'Achenbrite apologise for the interruption in service,' said a calm voice.' 'Please stand by.'

NINE

'Tosh? Toshiko!'

Gwen was starting to wish she'd listened more closely to the Torchwood health and safety briefing. At the time it had seemed too remote from real life, literally incredible. Police training had taught her the ABCs of basic first aid – A for Airway, B for Breathing, C for Circulation. The Torchwood equivalent seemed to go through the entire first half of the alphabet, and it started 'A for Alien, B for Bioform'. She'd sort of switched off by the time Ianto had reached 'I for Inseminoid'.

Here she was now, faced with an injured colleague, on the freezing rooftop of a shopping mall. Better to go with her police training. She was just about to roll her friend into the recovery position when Toshiko – thank God – seemed to revive.

'Steady, don't get up too fast.'

'Banged my head,' Toshiko groaned at her. 'How did you know where to find me?'

'What, apart from following a trail of blood and body parts, you mean?' Gwen held up her PDA. 'When I couldn't raise you on comms, I got a trace on your GPS coordinates. You were very insistent that we all get the hang of this.'

Toshiko gingerly levered herself up on her elbows and smiled. 'You're my favourite pupil.'

'Took a little while to get right,' Gwen admitted. 'Bit of interference. I may have tuned it to Red Dragon FM at first.'

'Interference? Of course! Are they still here? The men in uniform.' Toshiko sat up suddenly, trying to look around. The effort made her giddy.

'It's all right, Tosh. All the security staff have evacuated. Those that are still alive,' she added darkly.

'Different uniforms.'

'Well, there's only us here now. Rhys is down in the mall. Spitting feathers, of course, 'cause I wouldn't let him up here. I left him talking to Andy Davidson.'

'PC Andy,' said Toshiko. 'Cardiff's finest. Ouch!'

'Steady.' Gwen supported Toshiko into a proper sitting position, and examined the back of her head. 'Better get you back to the Hub, Tosh. Don't know how long you were unconscious. Need to get Dr Harper to look at that.'

Toshiko was getting agitated again. 'And Owen, too! We were talking on mobiles, and the line was disconnected by… the same people who were up here! Achenbrite, that was the name. I saw it on their uniforms.'

Gwen reluctantly allowed Toshiko to stand. 'Do you a deal. You can research Achenbrite. But you do it back at the Hub, and get this seen to.'

Toshiko gripped Gwen's arm. 'I need to show you something first.'

The fire alarm died just as they re-entered the building. Gwen sent general manager Maddock on his way back downstairs for some fresh air, which left her and Toshiko to examine the security room unaccompanied and unhindered.

She hadn't seen this much blood in one place since the space whale at that makeshift slaughterhouse. Only this was human blood and remains. She wasn't sure whether to feel ashamed that this made it so much worse. Easier to imagine these men with families, she supposed. Someone would have to tell their kids, or their neighbours, or their lovers. Thank God it wasn't her who had to do that any more.

'I saw the creature that did this,' Toshiko explained shakily. She picked her way carefully through the room, showing Gwen the incontrovertible evidence of scratches and splinters. 'A bat the size of a dog.'

'Like the thing I saw in the loading bay!' breathed Gwen.

Toshiko nodded carefully. 'It had a bullet wound in one wing. This was the same creature that killed your Weevils.'

'How did it get up here, then? Surely it would have just flown off. Not come back into the mall.'

Toshiko indicated the breakage around the door jamb. 'It didn't break in. It fought its way out. This door has a cipherlock on it. But those poor victims would hardly let that creature in and then lock themselves inside with it, would they?' Gwen saw the realisation dawn on Toshiko's face. 'Hey, remember how it vanished?' Toshiko manipulated the control desk, carefully avoiding the spattered blood. The central monitor switched to a view of the loading bay.

'No!' Gwen found it hard to believe, but the evidence seemed to fit. 'It came *through* the CCTV?' She studied the flickering image of the loading bay. She brushed at some shreds of plant that were partially obscuring the monitor screen. And was surprised to find they were attached to it. Growing in the cracked plastic casing. 'Look at this.'

Toshiko took an evidence bag from her pocket, and plucked some of the plant from where it was growing. 'There's no daylight in here. Not much natural light in the whole mall, that's why the greenery is all fake. So how's this growing in here?' The variegated leaf had also established itself between the carpet tiles. She pulled up one tile, and found the roots went into a crack in the screed concrete floor. 'This isn't your typical office plant.'

'And it's dying. See? The leaves are browning. Not watered enough, eh?' Gwen shook herself. What was the matter with her? She was standing by the bloody remnants of two men, and talking about plant care. 'This whole thing's going to take a lot of explaining,' she concluded.

'I know,' agreed Toshiko. 'And there's still those dead Weevils in the basement.'

'We're stretched too thin,' snapped Gwen. 'Just five of us. Torchwood doesn't have enough people.'

'What would ever be enough?' Toshiko prised a further plant sample from the base of the control desk, a double-headed bud that had not yet opened. 'Well, this'll be one of those things that needs covering up *afterwards*. Destroy the data trail in a week or so, once we know what the authorities *think* they've found. And if they can't work out what they've got, then there's nothing for us to cover up. Whoa!'

Toshiko staggered a little. She had risen too quickly from her crouched position.

'OK,' Gwen told her briskly. 'You need to get back to the Hub. Don't drive, get a cab. Use the account.'

Toshiko sighed. 'A secret organisation with a taxi account.'

Gwen grinned. 'Another Ianto innovation. It's in the name of Dr John Smith. Some in-joke of Jack's, apparently.'

'Bloody Andy Davidson!' Rhys the Rant was in full flow as they ascended the escalator. It was stationary, so they huffed up the big steps together. 'I've a good mind to cancel his invitation!'

'He hasn't replied yet,' Gwen tutted. 'Don't suppose you thought to ask him.'

'You're joking me.'

'What's he done now?'

This was all the excuse Rhys needed to go off on one. 'I was kidding about with him that I hadn't got the right change for the car park ticket. And he was banging on about how I'd get a sixty quid fine. And I was… Oh, what are you laughing at?'

Gwen had her fist in her mouth to stifle her giggles. 'He's having you on, love.' She shifted nearer and kissed him on the forehead. 'Right, was it this floor?'

Rhys hopped off the end of the escalator and crooked his arm for her to join him. 'We should shop more often when it's like this, eh?'

'That's 'cause the police have cleared the place. See how they've turned off the up escalators? Gets people out faster.'

Rhys looked around the deserted top floor. 'It's a bit spooky with no one here.'

'You sound like Andy.'

'Don't start,' he laughed. 'OK, I remember these Halloween decorations. There, in the far corner: Leonard's Toys and Games.'

The lights were still on inside the shop, bright behind the pumpkins and gravestones in the window. Its metal shutter was almost down, with just a metre gap at the bottom. The pair of them stooped beneath it.

'Oh my God!' Gwen's shock turned into relieved laughter. She'd seen the tall figure by the tills, like an over-tall Weevil. In the split second before she'd realised it was a dressed-up shop dummy, her gun was in her hand and pointed unwaveringly at its head. She holstered it again, noting that Rhys's face registered something between shock and admiration.

The empty shop had a locker-room smell, as though a football team had recently vacated it. A forlorn-looking papier-mâché diorama, painted and laid out like a battlefield, filled a section at the rear. Several carved figures had tumbled, discarded or forgotten, next to a couple of dice that had more than six sides. A handful of dog-eared MonstaQuest cards were strewn on the far side of the table.

Gwen rotated the blister packs that hung on wire racks by the till. She definitely recognised a couple of miniature Weevils and a Hoix – though the packaging called them 'Toothsome' and 'Maymer'. The other models were new to her, including one with two heads like snarling, spitting snakes. Another had a long tail and neck, with a horn in the middle of its forehead that made her think it looked like an angry diplodocus.

'We're closed,' snapped a thin voice. It belonged to an equally thin man, who stood up from behind the till counter, almost as though he'd been hiding there. The shopkeeper's dark hair spiralled wildly about his head. His abrupt appearance made Gwen jump involuntarily, which seemed to amuse him. He turned to face Rhys, and a look of recognition spread slowly across his face.

The shopkeeper's mouth twisted into what might have been a smile or a grimace. The tiny teeth and a wide expanse of gum made him resemble some kind of pasty boxer. 'Hullo,' he said, 'have you come back for your change, then?'

'Oh, aye,' Rhys laughed. 'Left in a bit of a hurry.' He offered his hand.

The shopkeeper started to fumble in his till.

'No,' laughed Rhys. 'I was introducing myself, proper like. I'm Rhys, and this is Gwen.'

'Dillon.' The shopkeeper shook his hand, and sheepishly gave him another gummy smile. He ignored Gwen. 'I remember. Gave me a tenner, for the MonstaQuest pack. Then hoofed it when the alarm went off. S'why I always take the money before I hand anything over.'

Rhys jerked his thumb in the direction of the main mall. 'You didn't evacuate with everyone else, then?'

'So many false alarms these days,' said Dillon dismissively. 'But I might as well close up the place now. Sales have been rubbish. But this – busiest trading day of the week? It might put me out of business.'

Rhys looked surprised. 'You said this MonstaQuest thing was really popular. Thought you must be coining it there, mate.'

'Not me. Gareth's the one making all the money on this. I'm just a niche supplier.' He pronounced it to rhyme with 'hitch', and spat the word like it was a curse.

'This is what we came to talk to you about,' interrupted Gwen impatiently. She pushed a 'Toothsome' blister pack across the counter.

'Seven ninety-nine,' said the shopkeeper.

'I thought you were closed?' Gwen replied, irritated by the misunderstanding. 'But I'm not buying.' She was aware that Rhys was scowling sidelong at her. Well, what did he want? He'd be chatting with this guy all day and getting nowhere. 'Where did these models come from?'

'Who wants to know?'

'Trading Standards.'

The shopkeeper's lips set in a narrow line. 'You can sod off then.'

Rhys blew out a sigh. 'Nice one.' It took Gwen a moment to spot that he was muttering at her. 'Please, Dillon. We need your help.'

'Oh, you're Nice Cop, are you?' The shopkeeper looked between them warily. 'You don't scare me.' His till snapped shut with an emphatic bang. 'Told you, we're closed. You can see yourselves out.' And with this, he was off to the rear of the shop, where he began to tidy up the papier-mâché landscape.

Rhys put his hand on Gwen's arm to stop her rushing after the thin man. He joined the shopkeeper at the diorama, and began to put model Weevils into a box while Dillon scooped up the scattered MonstaQuest cards from the painted surface. 'Come on, mate. What harm can it do?'

'What do you care?' muttered Dillon

Gwen could hear in Rhys's voice that he was struggling to keep calm. 'What about this Gareth? Got an address for him? Where can we find this mate of yours?'

Dillon snatched a Weevil model from Rhys's fingers. 'He's no mate of mine. Not any more!' he shouted. Gwen was alarmed to see the tendons sticking out in the shopkeeper's thin neck. MonstaQuest cards quivered in his fist – a couple of growling Weevils, and a fiery monster than looked as inflamed as Dillon's veined forehead. 'He talked me into setting all this up. Organised these table-top games. Such big plans we had. But when I tell him that the mall management have put the rent up, and I might have to close, what's he do? Storms out, that's what!'

Rhys gestured to calm the man down, but this just

infuriated him more.

'Left me holding the baby, good and proper! Niche supplier not good enough for him. He's getting MonstaQuest into Wendleby's. Right in the centre of town.'

Rhys gave Gwen a brief look of desperation. But Gwen wasn't really looking at him now. She was staring at the cards in Dillon's grip. There was a distinctive lick of fire from the flame monster. Dillon noticed where Gwen was focusing, and took a look himself. He squealed in surprise, and dropped the burning card onto the painted landscape.

It was as though he'd dropped a match onto petrol. With a whumph of ignition, a huge gout of flame spurted upwards from the landscape. All three leaped away from it as the intense heat seared them. This was no ordinary fire. It curled and twisted at the edges, until it defined a distinct humanoid outline. One arm reached out lazily, and a shelf of comic books burst spontaneously into flames.

Gwen's first reaction was to pull out her handgun. Rhys goggled. 'What the hell good is that?' he yelled. 'Dillon, where's your fire extinguisher!'

Dillon seemed frozen in shock. Another shelf full of magazines exploded into orange and red and yellow. The whole of one side of the shop was ablaze.

Rhys pulled the shopkeeper away as the table containing the diorama collapsed. The fire creature stood tall in the middle of the conflagration, and reached out a scorching tendril towards them. Dillon covered his face in horror.

A cold dark hole seemed to open up in the centre of the fire creature's torso. It folded its arms towards its body and bowed its head. Its furiously burning legs buckled, and the whole thing collapsed into a molten heap, scattering embers across the shop where they began fresh fires.

'It's gone!' yelled Rhys.

'But this fire hasn't!' called Gwen. 'We have to get out of here!'

They dragged Dillon out through the shop exit. After a panicky search, they located the crank that would bring the shutter fully down. Rhys ran to a fire alarm and managed to break the glass on the second attempt. The all-too familiar wail of the alarm echoed throughout the abandoned mall.

The Halloween masks and fake cobweb in the display were ablaze now, the windows blackening and cracking. Sprinklers were making a futile attempt to contain the inferno, but it was already clear that the fire was uncontrollable.

They'd backed away as far as the dead escalators when Leonard's Toys and Games blew out. Pea-sized chunks of window glass scattered across the area like a sudden shower. Within seconds, the pre-school store next door had caught alight.

Dillon sank to his haunches on the mall floor.

'That fire-monster enough to scare you?' Rhys asked him.

The shopkeeper began to sob. 'No one will believe me,' he wailed. 'They'll have me for arson.'

'Nah,' said Rhys. 'Spark from the till, wasn't it?' He nudged Gwen's elbow. 'We only just got you out in time, didn't we Gwen?'

'That's right.' Gwen helped Dillon to stand and indicated their escape route down the stairs. 'We're your witnesses.'

The shopkeeper had an incredulous, eager look in his eyes.

'Well, we could be,' added Rhys as they ushered Dillon through the fire doors. 'So long as we get this Gareth's home address.'

TEN

Ianto Jones looked at the snake, and the snake looked back at Ianto. Its jaw opened lazily, only twenty centimetres from his nose as he squatted. He could feel the tension in his haunches. He was going to have to stand up. Would that alarm the snake?

'*Oxyuranus microlepidotus*,' Jack told him.

Ianto didn't look away from the reptile poised in front of his face. He said calmly: 'You're making that up.'

'That's an inland taipan,' continued Jack, his voice low and dangerous. 'One bite contains enough venom to kill a hundred men.' He considered this for a moment. 'I dated a girl like that.'

'Well, some date *you've* turned out to be.' Ianto tutted and stood up with a groan. He pushed against the glass that separated them from the snake. 'All you want to do is talk about your former conquests, Jack.'

In the darkness of the reptile house's observation deck, Jack sought out Ianto's hand and squeezed it affectionately. 'You're a bit of a charmer yourself, Mr Jones.'

Ianto watched the taipan. It had already lost interest, and

slithered its olive-green body to the other side of the glass exhibit space. 'I didn't charm him. Or maybe her.'

'What d'ya expect?' Jack grinned. 'Staring out from a glass box for years on end. Who'd want that?' He nodded at the exit. 'C'mon, you can buy me an ice cream.'

They stepped out from the gloomy reptile house and into the cold, crisp, bright November air of Torlannau Zoo. The attraction had not long opened for the day, but already it was getting busy. Kids were chattering and screaming with delight at the antics of monkeys or horror at the smells of the hippos. Parents were already being pestered for ice creams. Zoo staff chaperoned and pointed, easily marked out in the growing crowds by their brightly coloured uniforms.

Ianto said, 'We keep Janet in a glass box. Down in the cells.'

'Never had you picked out as an animal liberationist.' Jack was pretending to look shocked. He checked the wristband above his free hand. He never seemed to take that damned thing off – not even in bed, though that did sometimes have imaginative compensations. Ianto suspected that Jack had only agreed with today's suggestion for a date at the zoo because Toshiko had mentioned some earlier Rift activity. And that ill-disguised glance was at least the tenth time Jack had scrutinised his wrist readout. He probably thought he was being surreptitious.

'You're off duty, Captain Harkness.' Ianto tugged Jack's hand, as though he could drag him away from work. 'Hey, what's the collective noun for…' He looked around for a nearby display area. 'Yeah… meerkats?'

'Is this a date or a pop quiz?'

'I'll take that to mean that you don't know,' persisted Ianto, pulling Jack into the walkway and the conversation at the same time.

'Or don't care.'

'Anyway, the answer is "a mob". How about… lions?'

'Easy! A pride. Like lions and cheetahs and all those pack animals.'

'Pack animals carry things,' Ianto objected. 'Y'know, beasts of burden.'

'Or they live in packs,' noted Jack. 'Y'know, like the word suggests.' He grinned at Ianto, and swung his hand forward. 'No, no, it's my turn. How about… Weevils?'

Ianto considered this briefly, before concluding: 'It's a shitload, obviously.'

They both laughed vigorously at this. An old couple were walking past them on the tarmac path. The pair had their collars turned up against the cold, hands shoved well into the pockets of their matching beige anoraks. The little old guy narrowed his eyes at Ianto. 'Language, please!' he said mildly. 'There are children about.'

'Sorry, sir,' said Ianto, trying not to laugh more. Jack wasn't helping by stroking the hairs on the back on Ianto's hand with his fingers.

The beige anorak studied them. 'You're a bit old to be holding hands.'

Jack smiled pleasantly. 'You have no idea.'

The elderly woman took her hand from her coat and tugged at her husband's sleeve. 'You're never too old to hold hands, Walter,' she chided him gently. 'You just carry on, boys.'

Walter's face relaxed into a smile, and he and his wife walked on down the path, their translucent fingers now intertwined in an affectionate knot.

'It's not a pack of leopards,' began Ianto.

Jack groaned. 'Are we still on that?'

'Or tigers…'

'Hey, we're near the tigers. Let's ask.' Jack had spotted a big guy in a grey boiler suit. Had to be one of the zoo staff. 'Hello!' Jack called to him. 'Do you know what you call a whole loada tigers? Like a crowd, or a pride, or…?'

The boiler suit barely registered them. He was a huge, tall guy. Maybe two metres from his solid mud-caked combat boots to the tip of his spiky red hair. A ginger wardrobe of a man, whose huge hands dwarfed the PDA he was manipulating.

'D'you mind?' Jack was insisting.

Ianto had walked over to join him. 'Not one of the zoo staff,' he said. He'd spotted that the crossed-keys logo on the man's grey uniform read 'Achenbrite'. The zoo uniforms, now he came to think of it, were blue-and-yellow.

The huge ginger guy snapped his PDA shut with a twitch of his sausage fingers. He hared away off the tarmac path, giant strides eating up the expanse of grass between the animal displays. A flock of flamingos startled and strutted away across their pen in a pink cloud of anxiety.

'Achenbrite?' mused Jack.

'I noticed,' agreed Ianto. 'Did you spot the earpiece?'

A shrill scream cut across the still air. It came from the opposite direction, and it wasn't the exhilarated squeal of a kid spotting a giraffe. This was full-throated terror. Ianto considered the directional signs, orienting himself with location information before running. There was the scream again. The signs indicated it came from over by the big cats.

Jack chased after him up the incline towards the Bengal compound. 'Did you see that sign?' he grumbled. 'They spelled "tiger" wrong.'

Ianto tutted. 'It's *supposed* to be tiegr. God, how long have you been in Cardiff, Jack?'

'Long enough.'

'Long enough to have learned a bit of Welsh, that's for sure,' puffed Ianto.

Jack pouted. 'I promise to be fluent by the time you introduce me to your family.'

'Then you have plenty of time to learn,' muttered Ianto. They skidded to a halt in front of the tiger enclosure. Two blue-uniformed zoo staff were directing a nosy crowd of visitors reluctantly away from the area. The squat burly man with a moustache made of broom bristles was having more success than his lanky counterpart. Jack and Ianto got past him during this distraction.

Ianto shoved at the access gate. 'Shouldn't this one be shut when the other is open?'

'Gives you some idea about what's in here,' Jack said.

'What's that, then?'

'Nothing. The animals have escaped.' Jack was checking his wristband again, with no attempt to disguise it from Ianto.

Another young guy was in there ahead of them. He had his hair tied back in a lank brown pony tail, for all the world like a zoo animal himself. He was struggling to comfort a shrieking woman, also in staff uniform. 'It's gonna be all right, Bethan,' he was saying, repeatedly, like a mantra.

'No it's not gonna be all right, Jordy!' she yelled at him. Snot and saliva hung down from her puce face. 'The tiger's already killed Malcolm.' She gestured wildly to a bloodied heap by the tree at the centre of the compound. Pony-tailed Jordy wasn't able to look, and concentrated instead on Bethan. She was having none of it. 'I spotted his body when the enclosure wall disappeared.'

'Disappeared?' Jordy's voice was shrill with incredulity, until he remembered he was supposed to be calming her. He stepped over to the exterior wall and slapped its unyielding surface with the palm of his hand. 'It hasn't disappeared. See?'

'It came back,' she grunted, her voice low and emphatic. She stared at the wall accusingly, as though daring it to be there in defiance of everything she'd said. Ianto followed the curve of the enclosure wall with his eyes. Beyond the moat that encircled the compound was an enormous glass observation window. Through it, Ianto could see that members of the public were being hustled away from the area.

Jack nudged Ianto to get his attention. 'The ground in here is sodden.' He was doing that thing he enjoyed – talking through the evidence as he took it in, encouraging confirmation or contradiction from Ianto. 'The pool in the middle there has overflowed. Backing up from the drain, maybe? Or was the victim hosing the place down before he got attacked?'

'Unless it's the tiger?'

'That's a lot of tiger pee,' muttered Jack.

A public announcement was echoing faintly on the still air. All the loudspeakers were in the main pedestrian thoroughfares, but some of the words carried into the tiger enclosure. The zoo was closing, and visitors were requested to make their way immediately and calmly to the exit.

The big observation window allowed Ianto to see the arrival of two armed zoo staff, their tranquillising rifles unslung. Something about the window made Ianto take a closer look at the brick-and-concrete wall, or as best he could across the moat. That gap must be about five, maybe six metres wide.

'We should leave,' Jack said. He had covered over his wrist monitor again, and was ready to go.

Ianto studied him curiously. 'Can't we help?'

'Not our job,' snapped Jack immediately. 'We catch aliens, not escaped zoo animals.'

Ianto wasn't in such a rush to depart. 'See there? To the left?' He pointed to a line that ran parallel to the transparent wall of glass.

'A crack in the brickwork?' ventured Jack. He looked more closely. 'It's too clean to be a crack in the mortar.'

Ianto nodded. 'You heard what that woman was blubbering about. Someone removed that wall, let the tiger out, and then replaced the wall. She didn't imagine it. But they didn't get the alignment perfect, and you can still see the join.'

He was about to say more when a commotion beyond the large glass wall caught his attention. Whatever it was, the armed zoo staff immediately swung around, pointing their rifles cautiously. One of them waved frantically at the other nearby staff to get them to move back and away, while he began to move cautiously forward.

'We need to get a closer look at that wall,' Jack said to Ianto. 'This moat's too wide. Need to get around the other side.'

'No ice cream then,' sighed Ianto.

'What can I say?' replied Jack. 'I'm a cheap date.'

The pair of them ducked back through the double-gated exit from the tiger compound. Ianto kicked sand and straw and tiger shit off his boots on the second gate, and hurried around to inspect the wall beside the huge glass observation window. The last of the zoo visitors were meandering away from it, shooed off by blue-and-yellow zoo staff like so many straggling geese.

Ianto dismissed an aggressive zookeeper with merely a stern look. 'Where d'you think those riflemen were going?' he asked Jack.

'Tiger hunting,' replied Jack. 'Better watch out, Mr "Safety First".'

Ianto rolled his eyes. He and Jack were unarmed, because Ianto had made them leave their handguns securely locked in the SUV, and the SUV securely immobilised in parking section 'Rhino 6'. Instead of arguing, he studied the wall. The artificially straight vertical line through the brickwork was even clearer on this side. And half-buried in the dried mud at the foot of the wall was an irregular-shaped device of unfamiliar metal. 'Alien tech,' grinned Ianto, and began to speculate on what he might christen it.

'Wait,' Jack warned him, 'we're being watched. They'd drawn the attention of a small group that stood at a closed fast-food concession, next to the zebra enclosure. Ianto recognised the big ginger wardrobe who'd blanked Jack earlier. The guy was talking to three other big blokes, all of them in non-standard grey boiler suits. You could make out the crossed-keys motif even from this distance. Ianto turned his head to catch what one of them was shouting.

'… still unsecured! Never mind the damned tiger, get it. D'you hear me? Get it, collect the equipment, and get out.'

And that was the point at which the tiger ran past. It charged around the corner of the chain-link fence that surrounded the large zebra enclosure, hugging the lower rail like a racehorse entering the final few furlongs. It was an orange-brown blur, barrelling at them, running for its life. Or for theirs.

Ianto instinctively flattened himself against the wall. Jack interposed himself between the animal and Ianto. The tiger charged towards them, past them, and struck the plate-glass window of its former enclosure. The animal's beautiful head connected with a sickening crunch, and it reeled back and slumped down almost at once.

The four men in grey boiler suits watched dispassionately. That was strange. Another odd thing was that they each carried a small suitcase.

Armed zoo staff emerged from the other side of the zebra enclosure, and raced over to the stunned, bewildered big cat.

'The tiger's never been up close to the glass,' Ianto breathed. 'So it thought it could get through. Running for home. They must have spooked it.'

'*They* didn't spook it,' said Jack darkly. He had snapped open his wrist device again. 'There's more Rift activity.'

Ianto nodded. 'It'll be this alien tech here that— '

With a whistle of air and a whump of displaced grit, the bloodied carcass of a zebra slammed down onto the ground right beside them. Ianto jumped back to avoid getting sprayed. The animal's head had been ripped off, and blood continued to gout from the neck, staining the black and white coat with vivid new red stripes.

'*That's* a more likely explanation,' said Jack slowly, and pointed.

The chain-link around the field opposite quivered like a plucked string. The dead zebra had been flung right over it, fully twenty metres. And the alien monstrosity that had tossed it that distance began to howl. A hole further along in the fence revealed how it had got in. The remaining zebras were running in panicky circles on the far side of their paddock.

The monster was a nightmare creature of ragged scales. A ridge of plates ran from the tip of its thrashing tail until it bifurcated at the shoulders and ran to the crown of two independently swivelling heads. Each surveyed a different area of its surroundings, baring an impossible number of slivered teeth at the humans below.

The bruisers in the boiler suits leaped into sudden activity, snapping open locks on their cases. If they had any sense, thought Ianto, they'd be fleeing for the exits with all the other zoo visitors. Instead, they were coordinating their movements around the double-headed creature.

'It's a Brakkanee. Stay still,' Jack told Ianto in a low, insistent voice. 'It relies more on sound than sight.'

'No wonder that tiger fled in terror.'

Jack studied his wrist device. 'It's a killing machine. It could handle a whole pride of tigers and not get out of breath.'

'It's not a pride, it's an *ambush* of tigers—'

'Not *now*, Ianto!' And with this, Jack was haring off towards the zebra enclosure, staying on the grass verge to reduce noise.

Ianto chased after him. Jack didn't look pleased when he saw that he'd followed him.

'Maybe it's not as bad as it seems,' joked Ianto.

'Yeah, right,' hissed Jack. 'The big monster that slaughtered that zebra made a little mistake. It's really sweet and lovely and kind to smaller animals. What a pity that ninety-nine per cent of Brakkanee give the rest a bad name.'

The Brakkanee breached the chain-link fence, peeling it back as easily as a net curtain. One head loomed towards them, hissing.

Jack had already activated his ear-comms to call the Hub. Ianto tried to tune in and listen, until he remembered his earpiece was back in the SUV's glove compartment. Trust Jack to have conveniently overlooked his own.

'She's gone shopping?' Jack was saying incredulously. 'All right, send Owen then, if he's nearer.'

The Achenbrite boiler suits were removing equipment from long pockets in their baggage. Jack reached the big redhead, and asked him to move back to safety with an insistent: 'We're Torchwood.'

The bloke reached out one meaty hand and pushed it into Jack's face. 'Leave it. It's under control,' he said. He sounded Scottish.

Jack stumbled back from the shove. 'If this is under control—' he began.

One of the armed zookeepers fired her tranquilliser gun. The feathered pellet slapped into the Brakkanee's head, and hung stupidly from its scaled cheek. The huge head shook in irritation, swooped down, and brutally smashed against the zookeeper. She plunged into the low earth moat around the zebra enclosure.

Ianto scurried quickly and quietly to help her. The woman was dazed and confused. He pulled her bodily up the embankment. Further along from where she had fallen, Ianto could see an earlier human victim of the Brakkanee. The white hair and the crumpled beige coat meant it could only be Walter. His wife knelt awkwardly beside him, sobbing, her hand still clutching his as he lay splayed out on the dry earth.

The creature had sensed movement below, and swung its two dreadful heads in small arcs as it attempted to pinpoint Ianto's position. Jack had seen this, and threw himself forward, yelling wildly. The two heads flicked immediately in his direction.

The Brakkanee dipped one head and seized him by the left leg. Jack was snatched into the air, shaken like a chew toy, and flung aside. He tumbled down the chain-link fence and crumpled in a heap, his leg mangled beneath him. The other alien head cocked as it considered this new victim.

A grey-green mist began to envelop the Brakkanee. During the commotion, the Achenbrite men had managed to remove equipment from their suitcases and erect tripod-mounted rifles. These weapons had balloon-shaped barrels, and sprayed a fizzing cloud of energy that wrapped itself around the contours of the alien. The Brakkanee shivered, shimmered, and began to shrink. Within a minute, it was small enough for one of the Achenbrite men to cover it with his suitcase, then snap it securely shut with the alien trapped inside.

Jack lay motionless by the fence. Ianto's instinct was to run to him, but he overcame the urge. Jack would be fine. There were other priorities.

The Achenbrite men were storing pieces of equipment back in their cases, and barking orders to each other. Ianto walked stealthily back to the tiger enclosure while they bickered: 'You left *what*? Well, go and fetch it!'

The ginger guy looked surprisingly cowed for a big bloke. He was coming this way. Ianto had to get the device unburied before he got here.

The Achenbrite man saw what he was doing. 'No!' he yelled. 'Stop that!'

Ianto managed to scrape the mud away from the edge of the alien tech. He prised it loose, pulled it free.

'Put it down!' bellowed the other man, pounding towards him. The giant guy was practically on top of Ianto now. 'The defence system's still active!'

The alien device scorched in Ianto's hand. There was a fiery blast of heat and light, and everything went white, whiter, whitest. And faded away to silent black.

ELEVEN

Rhys followed the directions they got from the traumatised shopkeeper. He steered the Vectra straight through town, negotiating the Saturday morning traffic. Progress was slow, and he annoyed Gwen by cracking open a can of Coke he'd found in the glove compartment and slurping it noisily. 'What's the point of having cup holders if I never use them, eh?'

They were headed to an address in Rhiwbina, a suburban area of North Cardiff near to the golf course. Gwen called Toshiko, who was already back at the Hub. They'd managed to find Gareth's surname from the electoral roll for his address. Toshiko had pulled up the photos from Gareth Portland's university matriculation card and passport, and sent those to Gwen's PDA. A solemn boy, with long hair and high cheekbones, stared back at her with insolent green eyes.

Throughout the remainder of the journey, Gwen tapped her fingers irritably on her knees at every delay. A young mum wrestling a buggy across a pelican crossing. A kid on a bike steering from pavement to pavement across a T-junction without checking for cars.

A fire engine wailed past them, traffic falling away for it in a slowly rippling wave. Rhys pulled over to let the emergency vehicle through. Gwen tutted, but then apologised.

'I haven't got blue lights on this thing,' Rhys grumbled. 'Not fitted as standard on our company vehicles.'

Gwen ached for the device that Toshiko had installed in the SUV that would change traffic lights to green as they approached. 'Should have got the Astra when we had the choice,' she grumbled. 'Nippier about town in the rush. Easier to park, and all,' she added as they went past a space that was just too small to reverse into.

After a few minutes fiddling around with the Cardiff A–Z, Rhys parked around the corner from their destination.

'You're on a double yellow,' Gwen noted.

Rhys laughed at her as he slammed his car door. 'When did Torchwood worry about parking tickets?'

Gwen gave him her 'you'll-be-sorry' face and said: 'It would be abusing my position to get a ticket cancelled for Harwood's Haulage.' She crossed the street, and laughed at his momentary hesitation before he jogged to catch up. 'Had you going there,' she smiled.

Gareth's house was set back from the road, a large Victorian redbrick building with wide bay windows. A thick twist of dark smoke spiralled out of its tall, highly decorated rubbed brick chimneys.

Gwen's first assessment was that it would be difficult to approach the building covertly because of the noise they'd inevitably make over the gravel driveway. Once they got to the main gate, however, the need for stealth evaporated. There were tyre grooves, deep and wide in the pale gravel, where a fire engine had swung in off the road and charged towards the house. That smoke wasn't coming from the chimneys – the upper floor of the house was alight. The roof had slumped and collapsed like melted wax on the far side, bringing down a couple of bedrooms with it. The crew rolled up the corrugated side of their fire appliance and attached thick hoses.

'It's a day for this kind of thing, isn't it?' observed Rhys.

Flakes of paper and ash were lifted from the fire into the air, and fluttered down into the driveway. Rhys showed a couple of half-burned examples to Gwen. 'We found the right place.' The charred fragments were still recognisable as MonstaQuest cards. 'Just got here a bit late, eh?'

'I wonder if he printed and packaged them in the house?' pondered Gwen. She looked around, and spotted a dilapidated wood-framed garage that stood separate from the house against the tall pine hedge. 'Maybe there's more stored over there?'

A small group of nosy locals had already gathered to gawp at proceedings. Gwen approached them and listened in.

'Hell of a row,' said a woman in a pink dressing gown and slippers, who was holding court among her neighbours. She was clearly not the type to miss out on a local tragedy. Her bedraggled hair was half-fixed with curlers, like an impromptu crown. 'They say that she's still in there. She'll be burnt to a crisp by now.' This last observation was delivered with a mixture of horror and relish.

'Who's that then, Mrs Stackpole?' asked a mousy woman in the group.

Mrs Stackpole tilted her head regally towards her inquisitor. 'His girlfriend,' she explained condescendingly. 'The mother never liked her, apparently.' Her voice dropped as though she was imparting a top secret. 'Ideas above her station. Maybe that's what the row was about. Heard it from my bathroom window, when I was doing my hair.'

'Leaning out of your bathroom window, more like.'

'It overlooks the far side of the house,' retorted Mrs Stackpole. 'Can I help it if there's shrieking and banging and Lord knows what other commotion? They were shouting fit to raise the roof, I shouldn't wonder. And blow me down, if the roof doesn't actually fall in! I thought it was an explosion.'

'That'd be the bolt of lightning,' piped up a thin woman in a tartan coat.

Mrs Stackpole didn't appreciate the interruption. 'Lightning indeed, Mary. There's not a cloud in the sky.'

'I saw it myself, from across the way,' insisted Mary.

Mrs Stackpole pouted in disbelief. 'Well, *I* was the one who dialled 999 straight off, wasn't I?' Her voice trailed off as she saw Gwen earwigging on the conversation. 'Can I help you, love?' she asked snappishly.

Gwen favoured her with a big smile. 'I was looking for Gareth.'

Mrs Stackpole set her mouth in a grim line of apology. 'I'm sorry, my love. He and his girlfriend were in the house when it collapsed. Did you know him?'

'We were… supposed to meet him here on business,' Rhys improvised.

'Odd man,' continued Mrs Stackpole, her mask of concern slipping somewhat. 'Geeky, my Robert would call him. Gareth was strange when he was at school, and didn't change much when he was at university.'

'Kept himself to himself,' volunteered the mousy woman.

'Solitary, yes,' continued Mrs Stackpole relentlessly, unwilling to surrender the stage at this point. She nodded in the direction of the smouldering house. 'But I don't think there'll be much of him for the fire brigade to find—' She broke off. Something had caught her attention over by the house. Everyone turned to look with her.

Two firemen were rushing away from the collapsed building, hampered from running as fast as they evidently wanted to by the gravel drive and their bulky reflective uniforms. 'Get back!' yelled one of them as he rounded the fire engine. His helmet fell off the back of his head, but he did not stop to retrieve it.

'Oh my good God,' said Mrs Stackpole as she saw something that finally made her shut up.

Gwen shrugged off the fleeing fireman who tried to stop her, and slipped from Rhys's anxious grasp too. She moved closer to the extraordinary sight that was destroying the arched porch of the house.

It looked like an angry little diplodocus, about the size of a cow, thrashing its long neck from side to side. Ash and fragments of MonstaQuest cards continued to dribble down from above. That's when Gwen remembered where she'd seen this thing before. It was exactly like one of the MonstaQuest toys from the shop. That horn she'd noticed in the model was actually a third eye in the centre of its forehead.

She flicked on her PDA, and angled it towards the house. Her comms clicked online as she tapped her ear. 'Tosh? Are you back at the Hub yet?'

Toshiko's voice crackled. 'Yes I am.'

Gwen focused the PDA's viewfinder. 'Are you getting this?'

'I take it you're not in Jurassic Park?'

'No. Nearer to Heath Park.' Gwen could hear Rhys calling

her away now. The diplodocus swung its long neck in her direction and its mouth yawned wide. She backed off, but stumbled, twisted awkwardly and fell onto the path.

'What's happening?' asked Toshiko in her ear.

The little diplodocus took a couple of stomping footsteps towards her. Gravel squirted from under its feet like gunshots. Gwen threw up her arm to defend her face. Just as it was upon her, the huge creature was enveloped in a bright flash. Gwen instantly recalled what that woman, Mary, had said: a lightning strike. But there was no noise.

And when she peered out from beneath her own raised arm, Gwen saw there was no dinosaur any more, either.

She rolled across the gravel drive, desperate to see where the creature had moved, terrified that it might attack from behind. But it had utterly disappeared. Her wild look back to Rhys, further down the drive, showed that he and the others were just as baffled.

Before she could even speak, the noise of a revving engine broke the fresh silence. It came from the dilapidated garage. More revving. The squeal of wheels on concrete. The splintering crash of the rotted wooden doors.

A bashed-up red Ford Mondeo burst onto the driveway, knocking aside scattered gravel and chattering women. For an endless couple of seconds it seemed to be heading straight at Gwen, and she locked eyes with its determined driver. Long hair, high cheekbones.

At the last moment, Gareth Portland wrenched the wheel hard left and swept past her down the driveway.

Gwen ran in pursuit of the car, cutting the corner and gesticulating to Rhys that he should follow too. He pounded after her, calling a half-hearted apology to the fire crew and astonished neighbours.

A hundred metres down the main road, Gareth Portland had been held up by a reversing rubbish van, and was only now squeezing past it.

Gwen snatched the keys to Rhys's car from his protesting hands, and slipped into the driving seat. He was still complaining as she threw the Vectra into gear and squealed into the roadway.

'That was a dinosaur back there!' Rhys gasped. 'I know they've got a better class of pet in Rhiwbina, but that's just taking the piss. Hey, mind my paintwork!' He winced as Gwen shot through the narrow gap beside the rubbish truck. 'And why are we chasing that car? It's not like he's stuffed Barney in the back of his Mondeo.'

'I've no idea where that thing went,' said Gwen. 'But what d'you bet that Gareth Portland has something to do with it?'

Rhys had shoved the MonstaQuest cards into his pocket when they'd left the mall earlier. He tugged the pack out now, and started to riffle through the designs.

'We'll leave Tosh to do a trace on the dinosaur.' Gwen tapped at her comms to make the call.

Toshiko was unable to reply, however. Right at that moment, she was distracted by an intruder, and trying not to die. Abruptly, improbably, utterly unexpectedly, a diplodocus had materialised before her eyes and was crashing around the central area of the Hub.

TWELVE

A first great whoop of air as he pulled fresh oxygen into his lungs. There it was again – the synaptic buzz between nerve fibres, the phasic burst of neurons. An engine kicked into life from a cold start. His whole body ignited with that astonishing feeling, every atom of him tingling, the orgasmic rush of life, the euphoria of simply being.

Jack was back from the dead, for the thirteen-hundred-and-seventy-ninth time. Or thereabouts. He'd stopped counting properly after twelve hundred.

He pawed away the thin red blanket that covered his face. The material snagged on a gash across his forehead, pulling the scab away from the already healing wound. Fresh blood trickled down the side of his nose, and he blinked it irritably from his eye.

Time for the usual quick recce of his surroundings, and how he'd got here.

Location: he was lying on a gurney in small enclosed room, like a white box. Strong smell of antiseptic not quite masking the scents of old blood and vomit. An ambulance, then. Stationary, engine off, so it had either arrived or not left yet. No way to know how long he'd been dead this time.

Last things he remembered: the Brakkanee attack in the zoo… Ianto in its path… Jack throwing himself in the way… the jaws seizing him… savage pain in his left leg, a wild flight through the air, a final crushing pain in his neck as he struck the fence…

He sat bolt upright, clutching at the arm that held him.

'Steady, Jack.' It was Owen's voice. 'You're back again. Can't keep a good man down.'

It was difficult to detect what emotion Owen was feeling. Seeing Jack come back to life has hard enough, without knowing that you were condemned to a living death. Jack could suck in air and, impossibly, breathe again. For Owen, breathing was impossible.

Jack touched Owen's forearm as reassurance. He rolled his neck slowly, aware that he shouldn't rush too quickly until he was sure the break had healed – otherwise, he'd just die again, and that would slow things down.

'Situation report then, Doctor Harper. This ambulance reached the hospital yet?'

'Still at the zoo,' said Owen.

Jack threw back the blanket, and swung his legs to put his feet on the floor.

'Whoa there, Captain,' Owen said, and held him back gently. 'One fatal wound to the forehead, and I think you'll find…'

Oh, all right then, decided Jack – he *wasn't* putting his feet on the floor. His right foot, at best. Because the left was dangling by a thread of flesh and gristle. The Brakkanee had chewed practically right through the leg. Pain blossomed in the stump of the limb as blood began to circulate. A few fresh red spots dripped off the end and onto the ambulance floor.

'Don't worry,' muttered Owen, 'you'll live. Of course.'

The back doors of the ambulance opened, and a grumpy-looking paramedic stuck her plump face in through the crack. 'We all set yet?' She caught sight of Jack's irreparably mashed leg, and blanched. 'Christ almighty! Barry told me he was dead!'

'That was the other guy,' Owen told her, and jerked his head in the direction of the second gurney.

For the first time, Jack saw the other body. A stitched red ambulance blanket covered it, from the tip of the head right down to the upturned toes at the end of the stretcher. A broad figure, utterly still. 'Ianto?' he breathed.

'No,' said Owen firmly.

'Well, look at this man's foot,' the paramedic insisted. She indicated Jack's injury. 'We can't hang on here.'

Jack wiggled his stump, and the foot swung gruesomely on its gristly connection. 'Hang on, very good,' he said.

'No offence, mate,' said the paramedic. 'But we need to get you to Cardiff General.'

She was all set to come in, but Owen stood up to block her. 'I told you, leave it. Torchwood will make the arrangements. Don't argue,' he continued relentlessly over her renewed protests. 'Just get out and I'll get on with it.'

'Sure he was dead.' The woman looked daggers at Owen. He could tell from her eye line that she was also considering Jack's head wound. 'I'm a paramedic, you know, not a porter.'

'And I'm a doctor,' Owen told her. 'D'you wanna take it up with Mr Majunath at A&E?'

The paramedic backed down.

Owen nodded. 'Well, piss off out of it, then.'

The doors emphatically slammed shut. Jack winced, and clutched his ruined limb as another spasm of pain lanced right up it.

'That had stopped bleeding out when they found you. Hasn't started again since you came back, even though your heart's pumping again. You sure it'll… y'know…' He waved his fingers like a magician.

Jack looked at Owen's splinted fingers, knowing that they would never repair like he could. 'It'll take a while. And it'll hurt like hell.'

'What's the worst you've ever had?'

Jack considered for a moment. 'You don't wanna know.'

'Burned to a crisp in a fire?'

'You're a sick man, you know that?'

'Says the man with the detachable foot.' Owen narrowed his eyes thoughtfully. 'Could you survive going through a meat grinder?'

'Never been tempted,' replied Jack. 'God, that would really sting, wouldn't it? Still what doesn't kill ya just makes ya stronger.'

'Tell me about it,' muttered Owen. He examined Jack's dangling foot. 'Could have been worse. Bite from a Brakkanee, you could have contracted Alien Lifeform Injected Cerebral Encephalopathy.'

'A.L.I.C.E.' Jack pondered this. 'Is that bad?'

'Nasty,' Owen told him. 'Christopher Robin went down with it.'

'I swear to God, Owen, sometimes I don't know what to believe with you.' Jack considered the body on the other gurney. 'If that's not Ianto, then where is he?'

'Dunno,' said Owen. 'Tosh sent me straight here. SUV was still in the car park. Rest of the place is evacuated, so it was easy to find you. I just followed the ambulances. Hell of a day for them, there's a shopping centre on fire on the other side of town and a major RTA in the centre of Cardiff. No sign of Ianto,' he concluded. 'It's like he's just vanished.'

'So who's the stiff?'

Owen tugged back the blanket. Jack knew the face at once. It was the ginger guy, one of the Achenbrite team. His neck lolled awkwardly on the thin pillow, a wide gash right across his pallid, freckled forehead.

'Got caught in an explosion. Whacked his head into a brick wall, smacked right through the skull, frontal and right sphenoid. But that's not the best bit.' Owen slid the blanket the rest of the way off the body.

The top half of the corpse was still in the grey Achenbrite uniform, somewhat bloodied from the brutal head injury.

The lower half, below the waist, was gone. Owen flicked the red cover back over, and the contours of the legs reappeared, like a magic trick. He removed the blanket once more, and the legs were gone again.

'Not amputated,' said Owen, 'just absent. What do you think about that?'

The tang of blood caught in Ianto's mouth. He turned his head, and suffered a brief moment of panic as water covered his nostrils. He coughed, and now the taste of brackish water choked him. He struggled and floundered until he somehow managed to drag himself into a shallow part of... wherever this was. Even as he spluttered, he could barely hear himself. He wanted to shout, but didn't know where he was.

Why was it so dark?

A profound darkness. He'd been down a mine shaft once, and his guide had extinguished all the torches and helmet lights. That kind of darkness. The utter absence of light.

Was this death? He'd half-joked with Owen about what there was after life. Owen had sneeringly told him he wouldn't understand, but Ianto had seen in his eyes that Owen really didn't want to talk about it. Maybe Ianto was discovering it for himself. Finding out what was there.

What waited in the dark.

He called out hopefully. His own voice was a dull hum in his head. His throat felt ragged. Was he whispering or screaming?

He opened his eyes wide. Nothing. But there was the buzz in his ears, and the taste of stale water in his mouth, and the scratchy sensation of angled concrete beneath him and water around his legs. When he ran his hands over his face, his shoulders, down across his outstretched legs, he could make out the contours of his own body and where the water lapped against him. There was a tenderness to his right side, and the clothes seemed torn. But he could definitely *feel*.

He choked back a sob of gratitude. And now he could hear that. The buzz in his ears began to resolve itself into meaningful sounds. Human voices in the middle distance.

'D'you hear that?' A young man's voice, Swansea accent.

A girl replying: 'If it's those bloody students, I will bloody 'ave them. Bloody rag week, it goes on for ever. The lazy bunch of pampered work-shy English bastards.'

The demotic sound of real Cardiff. Definitely not dead then.

'If they think we're paying a ransom for them to return that wall…' began the woman.

'Don't be stupid, Anna. How could they possibly have stolen a brick-and-concrete wall?'

'I've seen Derren Brown,' grumbled Anna. 'It's not my

fault *you* can't get Channel 4.'

The voices faded as the two moved further away. Ianto knew his hearing wasn't fading again, because now he could hear the sound of wind in the branches of a tree, the ripple of water around him. The throaty growl of a large animal close by.

Ianto's breath caught in his chest. He blinked furiously, hardly daring to move any further. He levered himself onto all fours in the water, some kind of shallow pool. Unless he could see, there was no way of knowing for sure what the animal was, where it lurked, or the extent of the danger.

He could guess, though.

The alien device had gone off in his hands. A defence mechanism, that's what the big bloke had been shouting about, wasn't it. Somehow, the blast had taken out the wall of the enclosure and hurled him into the display area. If he hadn't landed in the pool, the fall would have killed him. As it was, the device had somehow accelerated him away from what it perceived as an attacker, and… what, blinded him? How did that make sense.

The darkness was dissipating. If Ianto concentrated hard, he could start to discern shapes in front of him. He was initially suspicious that it was an optical illusion, his brain struggling to cope with his loss of sight and inventing stuff for him to see. But no, there were definitely the contours of the tiger enclosure… the scratched sandy surface… the tree in the centre…

And, oh yes, the tiger.

Ianto took a terrified, shuddering inhalation through his nose. The tiger's head darted in his direction. But it did not move towards him. It lifted its shaggy striped head and sniffed the air suspiciously. Maybe being chased by a two-headed alien monster had taken its toll on the big cat's confidence, but Ianto was too scared to be convinced of that.

His earlier desperate scramble had brought him to the shallow side of the tiger's pool. Ianto shuffled backwards out of the water, painfully aware of the splashing, keeping his eyes fixed on the striped animal. The tiger stared balefully at the ripples in the water, as if they were the most fascinating things in the enclosure.

Ianto continued to retreat, never once looking away from the creature, alert for any sign that it was going to plunge into the water, or start a skirting run around the pool. He could smell dung as he reversed, and winced as he worked out that he had shuffled into a pile of tiger shit. Instinct made him look at where he'd placed his hands. He could see a brightly coloured photograph that had dropped, half-folded, into the pile. On closer examination, he saw it was an oversized playing card from something called MonstaQuest. On the card was an image so arresting that Ianto almost forgot about the tiger: it was a stylised illustration of the Brakkanee.

A quick glance up revealed that the tiger had settled back down, apparently losing any interest in the earlier movement. Ianto tentatively reached out to pick the card out of the dung.

He couldn't see his hand.

It should have been obvious immediately. But the return of his eyesight and the distraction of the big cat made his realisation all the more shocking.

He couldn't see any of his body, any of his clothes. Not even when he waved his hands in front of his face. Or rather, in front of where his face should be. He could still feel his limbs and torso and head, as a quick exploration with his hands now proved.

Ianto uttered a laugh of incredulity, or maybe it was hysteria. The laughing hurt his ribs.

The noise made the tiger raise its head curiously, but it did not move. No wonder it couldn't locate him. Ianto Jones was invisible.

THIRTEEN

Toshiko sheltered in the lee of her own workstation as glass cascaded around her. She tried not to cry out, in case the dinosaur heard her.

She'd fled here as soon as the creature had materialised in the Hub. This was insane, she thought. There was no way it could have walked in. It was some kind of small sauropod, maybe a diplodocus, though the third eye suggested it was extraterrestrial. It certainly couldn't be a fully grown Earth dinosaur, otherwise it would have filled pretty much the entire space. It was still as big as a bull, and possibly as dangerous.

But it wasn't a carnivore. So did hiding make it more or less likely that she'd be killed? Would it notice if she made a noise? And even if it did, would it care?

The thing was stretching its long neck towards the upper-floor Hothouse. The room had been converted from the old Boardroom when they had conducted extensive repairs to the Hub, and was filled with potted plants, most of them alien in origin. Toshiko had been up there only a few minutes earlier, conducting research on the double-headed plant sample she had picked up at the mall. The room's bright illumination must have attracted the hungry creature to the tempting greenery within, and that's why it was straining to reach up to it.

An angry shriek echoed around the cavernous room, echoing off the tiled walls. Torchwood's own resident dinosaur was a pteranodon. Jack and Ianto had captured it some years previously, and allowed it free access to the Hub. Toshiko always worried that the pteranodon might be territorial, and had speculated on the risks of having their workstations covered in dinosaur droppings. Jack seemed unusually well informed about the territorial habits of a creature that hadn't existed on Earth for over seventy million years, but the pteranodon was house-trained, had never yet attacked a Torchwood employee, and didn't bring home any of the local sheep that it occasionally ate on night hunting trips. Nevertheless, the pteranodon was clearly very annoyed to find a rival in the Hub. It perched on the walkway outside the Hothouse, pecking at the top of the other dinosaur's head and screeching with rage.

The sauropod flicked its tail casually and cleared Gwen's desk. A flat-screen monitor cracked and split as it tumbled to the floor. Toshiko felt her own desk shiver with the impact. She let out a little yelp as its contents scattered onto her head – pens, her plush toy tiger, a mouse dangling on its cord, a couple of bon-bons from the jar that Gwen had bought her. She caught the photo of her parents, before it smashed on the metal walkway, and placed it safe and flat on the floor.

The sauropod shuffled sideways to fend off the pteranodon's enraged attack. Around its feet, sprouting through the metal grille of the floor, was a fresh growth of alien flowers. Half a dozen of them, yellow double-headed blooms. Toshiko had brought only one sample back, and that was now in a Torchwood evidence bag on her battered desk. There were no other samples like it in the Hothouse – she'd checked that earlier.

These new blooms had arrived with the dinosaur. But how had the dinosaur arrived, just materialising out of thin air?

The pteranodon screeched again. Toshiko craned her neck to look up, and saw it stretch its wings wide. She shivered. It reminded her of the monstrous thing that had attacked her at the mall.

Ah, the monstrous thing that had disappeared *into* thin air in front of Gwen. It had reappeared in the security room – where she'd found the double-headed alien buds.

Could the bat-creature have been transmitted through the CCTV signal? And could this dinosaur have been sent to the Hub through Gwen's PDA?

Toshiko levered herself up from behind her workstation, and clattered her fingers across the keys of her terminal, oblivious to the noise, no longer caring whether the sauropod heard her. With a few further deft keystrokes, she had closed down all the CCTV monitoring in the Hub. The dinosaur wasn't going to get transmitted accidentally to one of her unsuspecting colleagues.

On the other hand, it wasn't going anywhere, was it? The tail swished irritably, and flung Gwen's workstation chair into the shallow pool at the base of the steel tower.

Toshiko tapped a couple of additional instructions into her computer, and heard the satisfying shunk sound of the Armoury door unlocking.

The dinosaur shuffled some more, denting the walkways,

and kicking the Armoury door as it opened outwards. Toshiko tried to assess which way the creature would move. The gap between its legs widened.

This would be like running across a motorway, only the risk here was deadlier.

Toshiko threw herself forward, hardly daring to breathe.

She practically fell into the Armoury. When she started to breathe again, she took in ragged lungfuls of air.

The Armoury rattled around her as the sauropod leaned heavily against the frame of the room. Toshiko stared at the racks, frantically trying to remember where the weapon was. For a dreadful moment, she wondered whether it had been removed by one of the others.

No, there it was: the Jamolean lance. She wrenched at it, catching her fingernails against the rack. The power pack had not depleted, she noted thankfully.

The Armoury clattered and shook once more. The pteranodon's defiant shriek echoed in Toshiko's ears. The sauropod's flank pressed against the gap where the door had been, and the whole frame began to buckle under the pressure.

Toshiko pressed the barrel of the weapon against the tough flesh of the dinosaur's hide, and pulled the trigger.

She could feel the heat from the energy weapon as it discharged into the creature's side. A protesting bellow of shock and pain roared around the Hub. She pressed herself back into the Armoury, sheltering as best she could behind the racks that held the alien arsenal, praying silently that the backwash of heat from the fired weapon would not detonate any of the others. In only a few seconds, the whole room had become as hot as a dry sauna.

The exothermic reaction started by the Jamolean lance

seared and burned around the Hub, until the sauropod collapsed into a smouldering heap. Toshiko stayed back for several minutes until the effect was completed. When she felt brave enough to venture out, the pteranodon was pecking at the shrivelled, charred remains. Toshiko was sure she could see a glint of Cretaceous amusement in those reptile eyes.

The whole Hub smelled of heat and charred flesh. Toshiko slumped into her workstation chair, and wiped the back of her hand across her perspiring forehead. She started to bring the CCTV back online, and smiled at the thought that her vanquishing of the creature had not been caught on camera. As she worked, she began to think what else might connect the creatures she'd seen – the bat-thing, this pseudo-diplodocus, even the Weevils… and then she had it.

It was that catalogue device they'd stored away some three months ago. After some thought, Ianto had named it the Vandrogonite Visualiser, though Jack had quibbled that just because it was found in the possession of a Vandrogon that didn't mean the race had manufactured it.

Toshiko decided that it was time to get the Visualiser from the Vaults.

FOURTEEN

The front wheels of the chair jarred against the ambulance door for the third time, and Jack gasped in pain. 'Sorry,' said Owen, who was steering. 'I'd usually ask a porter to do this.'

'I'm honoured,' winced Jack, who had insisted on getting into the wheelchair in the first place. He wanted to escape the ambulance before it left the zoo.

Owen warned him that the foot was 'hanging by a thread'. Except that he used medical terms that sounded like tendons or subcutaneous exposure or something. Didn't matter, thought Jack. Whatever it was called officially, it hurt like hell. And yet he had literally hopped into the seat of the chair, and urged them both out of the ambulance and onto the tarmac of the zoo's main thoroughfare, in the face of Owen's objections.

The paramedics protested, too. The dumpy one, Brenda, had waved her credentials at Owen. Barry, the quietly spoken guy with the face like a disappointed horse, hovered morosely in the background, clearly reluctant to intervene beyond a token objection. Owen mentioned the word 'Torchwood', but Jack thought it was probably the sight of his holstered

SIG P228 semi-automatic that persuaded them to stop hassling him. Owen casually exploited their discomfort by commandeering their ambulance. He strongly implied that the dead body constituted a biohazard, but that he and Jack were at liberty to leave – Jack lost track of the clinical jargon that Owen tossed at the cowed paramedics. As a triumphant conclusion, he told them to confirm it with Control back at Cardiff General.

Bumptious Brenda and by-the-book Barry seized on this like drowning swimmers grasping a lifebelt. Which in turn gave Owen the opportunity to reroute their radio call to the Hub. Toshiko swiftly substantiated everything that Owen had said. Verbatim, in fact, because he stood behind them and fed it directly to her from his PDA.

'What are we gonna do about getting back to the General?' Brenda bleated at Owen, once her call had finished.

Owen waved airily, a gesture that encompassed not only the other injured zoo visitors being treated at the scene, but also a couple of other ambulances that had parked nearby. 'Plenty of other people to assess here. After that, get a lift from another crew.'

Barry shrugged. Brenda was opening her mouth for a fresh remonstration when a shout from a paramedic took her over to another victim. There were two stretchers. On one, a grey-faced, white-haired woman was receiving oxygen. The second stretcher's occupant was overlaid with a stitched red blanket, but the corpse's arm had slipped from beneath it. The arm dangled free for a moment, uncovered. From the gnarled finger joints, Jack could see that Walter and his wife had finally been parted.

Owen got the collapsible chair down from the rear of the ambulance, and wheeled Jack away from prying eyes. They ended up in a secluded area to the side of the reptile house, far from the milling crowd of rubberneckers and emergency staff, and Jack was able to call back to the Hub.

'Tosh, what have we got on Achenbrite? If you can hack into the zoo's CCTV, you might get some visuals on them.'

'On the whole, I'd rather not,' said Toshiko's voice in his ear. 'And you know that "CC" means "closed circuit". They're not on an accessible network. You might as well ask me to hack the contents of one of their filing cabinets.'

Jack pondered this. 'Those Achenbrite guys had a logo on their overalls. Crossed keys. Like the Papacy, but without the crown.'

'I've set off a search now.'

Jack grinned. 'Brilliant, as always. And Tosh – great job convincing the ambulance crew on that call they made.'

He could hear in her voice that she was smiling too. 'Think of me as the fourth emergency service.'

'I rely on you in a crisis, you know that.' Jack could hear something else in her voice too. 'Are you OK? Sounds like you're gasping for breath.'

'It's been a busy morning for me.'

'Unless,' Jack suggested, 'this is one of those dirty phone calls?'

'That's not the kind of emergency service I had in mind,' tutted Toshiko, and Jack could picture her disapproving frown. 'I thought I'd move some of the furniture around. You won't recognise the place… Here you go.'

There was a computer bleep as her search results arrived. Jack shaded the display monitor on his wrist monitor with a cupped hand, and squinted at the miniature image.

In comparison with their surroundings, even on this reduced scale, the familiar grey-suited figures were brutally large. The video surveillance images showed that they were corralling a barking pack of dogs around a block of low, flat buildings. 'You're showing me a rerun of *Animal Rescue*?' Jack said.

'Seemed like nothing important at the time. They recaptured nearly a hundred animals after a mass breakout from a breeding kennels in Lisvane. The Torchwood systems flagged it as insignificant because it was just domestic animals, not aliens.' Toshiko caught her breath again. 'We only tagged it at all because there was contemporaneous Rift activity.'

'Probably the alien tech they used. But no signs of them capturing extraterrestrials?'

'Not unless they were disguised as border collies.'

'You'd be surprised. All right. Thanks, Tosh. And don't put your back out.'

There was the briefest of pauses before Toshiko said, 'Pardon?'

'Moving furniture,' Jack explained as he signed off. 'Leave the heavy lifting to Ianto. He's a bit of an expert.' He looked around, levering himself up a little on the arms of the wheelchair. 'Owen, where *is* Ianto?'

'Dunno, mate,' Owen said, and holstered his weapon. No point in drawing unnecessary attention. 'I thought you were in a rush to get out of that ambulance 'cause you knew where Ianto was. I told you, I just followed the blues and twos.' Here he indicated a couple of police officers who were directing members of the public to leave the zoo and discouraging stragglers who had not yet evacuated.

Owen was saying something else, but Jack didn't hear it properly. He was distracted by the sight of someone else. 'Gimme a break,' he muttered, and shrank into the wheelchair.

David Brigstocke was picking his way across the grass verge towards them. He showed his Press pass to one of the police officers. The PC was more occupied with a weeping woman, and nodded Brigstocke on. The journalist had one hand in the pocket of his cheap check jacket. No doubt clicking on his digital recorder as he prepared to accost Jack once more.

'Who's your friend?' Owen asked Jack.

'David Brigstocke, BBC Radio Wales.' The journalist offered a handshake that Owen did not accept. 'And yet, I know *you*, Dr Harper. Born fourteenth of February 1980. Recruited into Torchwood in—'

'Yeah yeah,' interrupted Owen. 'Tell me something I don't know.' He grabbed the handles of the wheelchair, but was unable to manoeuvre Jack away because the newcomer had placed his feet directly by the front wheels.

'All right.' The journalist spoke directly over Jack's head, staring intently at Owen. 'I know you were involved in that fatal shooting at the Ostelow Academy last February. On your birthday, too – don't you get any time off? The "Valentine's Day Massacre", that's what the *Western Mail* called it. Only they didn't have any pictures of the fish-headed alien that started the brawl. Torchwood did a pretty thorough cover-up.'

'You're the one who's fishing,' Owen replied calmly.

'No casualties, either. All tidied up by your colleague, Mr Jones, no doubt.' Brigstocke flicked a glance down at Jack. 'Nice to see him earlier today. Is he around?'

Jack kept his face neutral.

'Or perhaps,' continued Brigstocke casually, 'you got your mates in Achenbrite to handle that? I saw them here earlier.'

Jack stiffened at the name. He groaned inwardly as soon as he saw that Brigstocke had registered his involuntary reaction.

'You gonna get out of our way?' Owen asked in a dangerous tone. 'You could be a casualty, Mr Brigstocke. Hit and run by a wheelchair.'

Brigstocke stood his ground, still smiling. 'That wouldn't be a threat, would it, Dr Harper?'

Jack gestured to Owen not to respond. 'It's OK, Owen. I can handle this.'

The journalist snorted. 'Handle me, you mean?'

Beneath the ambulance blanket, Jack's foot throbbed and he wanted to shout at the pain. Instead, he gritted his teeth and tried to smile politely. 'Now is not a good time, Mr Brigstocke.'

'When would be a good time, Captain Harkness?'

'Kinda busy right now. Dr Harper is taking care of me…'

Brigstocke offered another sarcastic handshake to Owen. 'I should congratulate you, because you've worked miracles on this patient.' His humour seemed to be dissipating, though. 'I saw your injuries, Jack. All right, that head wound looked worse earlier than it does now. But they covered you over with the sheet, I saw that. They thought you were dead, and they're supposed to be the experts. Paramedics don't make mistakes like that.' A harder, more insistent tone had entered his voice. 'So, would it be fair to say that your deadly injury has healed? The whole world would marvel at that, wouldn't they, Jack?'

Jack put his hands on the wheel rims of the chair to indicate that the conversation was over, and he was ready to leave. 'Another time.' He clamped his teeth together, and began to roll the chair across the tarmac walkway. Owen paced behind him, but Brigstocke scuttled alongside.

By the time he'd reached the police line, Jack had abandoned any hope of escape.

Brigstocke dropped to his haunches in front of the wheelchair. 'Why won't you give me the time to talk about Rhodri?' He placed his hands on Jack's knees like a supplicant. A jolt of fresh agony sparked through Jack's limbs and he stifled a yell. 'You can tell me what happened to him. Not for a news story, Jack. But for his family. For his friends.' His voice caught in his throat. 'Yes. And for me.'

'Dunno what you mean.'

'Don't lie to me, Jack! I've seen what's been going on here at the zoo today.'

'Yeah. It's a tiger escape. Nasty business. Panic. Lot of people got hurt.'

'I followed you here, you idiot! From Holy Innocents. I *saw* that thing. That was no tiger. What else have you got concealed in this place – a flying unicorn maybe?'

Jack blew out a long sigh. 'Sorry, David. I really can't help you. And I think you kinda know that.'

Unexpectedly, Brigstocke yelped and jerked to his feet. He was holding his hand behind him for some reason, like he'd been kicked in the butt.

The policeman behind him staggered. His peaked cap dropped off, though he managed to catch it and replace it on his head. 'Steady, sir,' he said to Brigstocke, and resumed his calm conversation with the distressed woman.

No sooner had the cop turned away again than his legs buckled and he dropped to his knees. His cap flipped right up into the air, and then shot across the walkway as though thrown there. Jack heard a filthy insult uttered in Welsh and a slapping sound. The cop reacted by snapping his hand to his own face. When he turned round angrily to confront his assailant, he glared angrily at David Brigstocke. An angry red mark was already showing finger marks on the cop's cheek and neck.

'All right, sir, I think we've had enough.'

Two more police officers confronted the bewildered Brigstocke.

Jack felt the wheelchair start to move briskly along the tarmac path and away from the scene. He turned awkwardly to ask Owen to take it easy. Owen was several metres away and watching the wheelchair propel itself away from him and up the gradient of the walkway.

The chair stopped, turned slightly, and applied its own brakes.

Jack sensed the gentle touch of a warm hand stroking his neck tenderly. Hot breath against his face. The soft caress of lips, the insistent pressure of an exploratory tongue parting his lips and flicking over his teeth. He'd know that kiss anywhere. He closed his eyes and surrendered to it. After a moment, he was finally able to gasp: 'Ianto!'

He grinned at Owen as he jogged up the path. 'You all right, Jack? It looked like you were having a fit. Ouch!'

'Careful,' Ianto's voice said from somewhere nearby.

Owen gaped at nothing. 'Oh, you are bloody kidding me!'

Jack's bellowed a huge laugh. 'The invisible man. I wish I could say I was glad to see you, Ianto. What happened?'

He heard Ianto give an exasperated sigh. 'I dunno. And unlike you, I can't tell how badly injured I might be. I think we should get back to the Hub. Get away from that journalist over there while he's occupied with the policeman that I clobbered.' Jack heard Ianto chuckle. 'Why I am pointing? You can't see me.'

Jack's wheelchair sprang forward again as its invisible driver steered it towards the zoo exit.

FIFTEEN

The Vectra took another corner too fast, and Rhys bounced off the side window again. He hated being a passenger; he always wanted to drive himself. He threw a wild look over at Gwen, but she'd given up apologising after the first three sharp turns had jounced him against his seatbelt.

She was engrossed in her driving. He could tell from the fierce concentration in her eyes. It was a steely focus that he recognised from home, the signal that she wasn't going to be distracted or dissuaded. She was in her 'all or nothing' mode. Either they would catch up with Gareth in his Mondeo, or Rhys was going to wake up in the remains of his own company car, enveloped by the air bag and ready to admire the efficiency of the Vectra's crumple zones.

When Gwen accelerated sharply between two badly parked white vans in a side street, Rhys couldn't help but wonder whether the object of their pursuit cared quite so much about passers-by and property. That grotty red Mondeo shouldn't be able to outrun this brand-new Vectra, except that its driver didn't hesitate about hitting other vehicles or, on one occasion, a pedestrian. Gareth shot down a residential street and dinged every parked car along its length. Wing mirrors littered the narrow carriageway, and an outraged chorus of car alarms brought even more outraged owners out to survey the damage.

'Do you think he's been on an *offensive* driving course?' asked Rhys. His teeth rattled almost as much as the contents of the glove compartment, where he'd stashed the MonstaQuest cards on his hurried departure from the mall. The half-drunk can of Coke from their earlier journey shuddered in its cup holder, slopping blobs of cola across the dash.

They sped along a wider stretch of roadway. A serrated row of white tick marks led up to the squat yellow shape of a speed trap. Rhys found himself stamping down with his right foot. He bit back a warning to Gwen, knowing it was futile. But he couldn't help giving a little groan when the double-flash of the camera told him they'd been snapped.

'It's me that'll get the ticket when they contact the leasing company,' he grumbled.

Gwen cackled. 'Like Tosh hasn't had to hack the ticketing database before!' She gave him the briefest of amused sidelong glances. 'There was this blowfish in a sports car, liked nothing better than racing an MX5 Eunos along the Gabalfa flyover…'

'I don't know what to believe any more,' Rhys replied. 'I used to think all them alien sightings were caused by terrorists putting psychotropic drugs in the water supply. This morning I've seen a dinosaur eating a house in Rhiwbina.'

The Vectra skidded left through a red light after the Mondeo. Rhys could hear the blaring horns and glass smash of the cars they left in their wake. Gwen crunched the gears down into third, and cursed as the engine over-revved. 'Oh, these boots!'

Rhys peered into the driver's side footwell. 'Bloody hell, Gwen!' he shouted. She was still wearing those long boots with the big heels that she so liked, the pair she wouldn't tell him the price of. 'How can you control this thing in those heels?'

'Didn't really have time to change before I got in.' Gwen jerked her head at the steering wheel. 'Want to have a go?'

'No need to be sarky,' replied Rhys. He clutched at the dashboard as his fiancée skidded his car through another red light. A cacophony of beeps and crunches told him all he needed to know about what they'd left behind them at the junction.

Ahead of them, the red Mondeo cut a sharp right across traffic. Oncoming vehicles screeched to an angry halt. The Mondeo clipped the rear wheel of a drop-handle racing bike and catapulted its rider onto the pavement in a tumbling dazzle of bright Lycra. Rhys winced. His instinct was to stop, get out and help. Even before he'd finished the thought, Gwen had flung the Vectra through the gap in the opposite line of traffic.

'Here we go,' she said with satisfaction. She pushed the stick shift into fourth and accelerated onto the dual carriageway. Rhys glanced over at the speedometer, and saw they were roaring up to 80.

They were gaining on the tatty Mondeo. Even though their target weaved an erratic path through the traffic, Rhys's new company car and Gwen's confident driving had the edge. 'Gareth is having to make decisions about what to do at every turn,' she told Rhys. 'We just have to keep pace.'

The Mondeo screeched onto the scrap of hard shoulder and vanished behind a high-sided fourteen-wheeler. From the TIR carnet and the registration, Rhys could tell it was a French camion. The rig wobbled and the strident horn resounded with the driver's outrage and surprise. Gwen tapped the accelerator and sped around the other side.

Gareth had ploughed on past the truck's nearside and down a slip road. They were going to overshoot and lose him. Gwen pressed hard down on the brake and pushed the Vectra into the path of the French rig.

'Jesus, Gwen!'

The horn brayed again, but this time there was an accompanying shriek of heavy tyres on the roadway. The French driver slammed down on his brakes and wrestled with the monster vehicle to avoid a collision.

The Vectra bounced over the white chevrons between the carriageway and the slip road, and the Mondeo was in their sights again. Gwen calmly shot out into the junction roundabout. Rhys could still remember the smell of burning rubber from the truck's tyres, and the sight of the driver's madly staring eyes in the cab.

The Vectra cut a corner, and jerked harshly up a high kerb. The whole car bounced, the can of Coke jolted out of its cup holder, and the contents of the boot rattled and bounced against the rear door. The door of the glove compartment dropped open and the contents barfed out over a startled Rhys.

Gwen gave an anguished cry of shock. She twisted the wheel in an effort to regain control.

'What's the matter?' bellowed Rhys, panicking and looking desperately around to work out what was happening. It wasn't only the movement of the car that shook him.

'Sorry, love!' Gwen gave a whooping gasp of relief as the car levelled again.

'I really thought we were going to overturn, or something. You scared me half to death there, Gwen.'

'That can of cola,' explained Gwen. She casually brushed the empty container into Rhys's footwell. 'Dropped into my lap, and it's soaked right through. Just look at the front of my jeans!'

'That's nothing,' muttered Rhys, calming down a little. 'You should see the back of mine.'

Traffic was thickening again as they came into the centre of town. Rhys began to recognise the roads that led into Cardiff Bay. Gareth wasn't afraid to veer onto pavements if that meant getting past a stationary vehicle. At one point he smacked against the Perspex and metal of a bus stop, cracked the transparent shelter and scattered a yelling line of people.

Rhys watched their quarry career over a Keep Left sign. The wheels lifted clear from the pavement as it scooted over the corner of a junction. With a high-revved whine, the car raced off towards the embankment. The Millennium Stadium peered across the river as the car jigged and danced madly ahead of them. That's where I want to be, Rhys told himself. Watching the international. Not chasing around Cardiff as a helpless passenger in my own bloody car.

Gwen roared up behind Gareth's Mondeo until they were right on his bumper. Rhys could see why the driving was more unpredictable than ever. Gareth was tossing back his long hair and raising something with his left hand.

'Look at him! He's using a mobile phone! That's…' Rhys was going to say 'dangerous' until he acknowledged how stupid that would sound. 'That's illegal,' he concluded lamely.

'Oh sure, Rhys,' laughed Gwen. 'Three points on his licence is *exactly* what he's worrying about.' She veered right as the

Mondeo slipped into a side road. 'And I'm not convinced that *is* a mobile phone.'

The thing in Gareth's hand was filling his car with bright light.

Coming down the narrow embankment carriageway towards them was a huge, growling pantechnicon. Its blank cab front stared them down, the impassive bulk defying them to continue. The square shape of its trailer loomed behind the cab, and the hiss of its air brakes made it even more like a bull about to charge.

'Ha!' crowed Gwen. 'You are going nowhere now, Gareth!'

The Mondeo's nose dipped and its brake lights flared. Gwen's leg jerked forward as her foot sought the brake, but the Vectra screeched into a short skid and smacked the rear of the car in front. 'Aww, no!' yelled Rhys as the bonnet crunched up.

The light from the Mondeo increased. Gareth's head and shoulders were a stark silhouette in the brilliance. Rhys blinked, thinking that the brightness was hurting his eyes. And shivered.

It had got very cold all of a sudden. He could see his own breath.

With impossible speed, a thick, freezing fog surged around the car. Frost patterns began to craze the front windscreen. Visibility had dropped to only a few dozen metres. Everything outside was rimed with ice – lampposts, parking meters, the road surface. A woman laden with plastic supermarket bags twisted, skidded, and fell headlong on the pavement. Her shopping spilled from the bags and over the slick surface.

Rhys heard the Mondeo's engine revving again. Gareth swerved the car hard right, his wheels spinning furiously to get traction before he jolted up over the pavement and through a low barrier on the far side of the street.

Gwen flicked on the Vectra's lights. And gasped at the sight through the windscreen.

The pantechnicon was slewing towards them. The driver grappled with the steering as he struggled to arrest the huge vehicle's progress, and the cab slowly twisted from side to side like an enormous animal sadly shaking its head in resignation. It wasn't going to stop, and the Vectra was right in its path.

Rhys grabbed for the door handle, but Gwen grasped his other arm. 'I see where he's gone!' she hissed. Put the Vectra back into gear. And bumped the wheels onto the far pavement and through the gap that Gareth's Mondeo had made in the fence.

Behind them, the pantechnicon slid on its unrelenting journey down the iced roadway, crunching against street lamps and tipping them over.

Rhys's relief was short-lived. The nose of the Vectra dropped, and the car breached the embankment barrier. The car see-sawed briefly on the edge, then careered down a steep incline.

'It's the river!' he yelled at Gwen. His voice quavered as the car bobbled and rattled its inexorable way over the uneven surface.

'I know!' she snapped back at him. 'Just look at it.'

The car plunged onwards, out of control. Shreds of bushes and skeletal branches clutched and scratched at the paintwork like talons. The fog around them gave the briefest glimpses of their surroundings. The chipped, angled embankment blurred past the side windows, changing from grey to green where the river had lapped and splashed up the base of the concrete.

A bone-crunching thump rattled Rhys's teeth in his jaw. At the bottom, instead of a splash as they hit the water, the car groaned and crunched when it struck the frozen river. The Vectra's engine whined as the wheels spun helplessly and the vehicle described a lazy circle on the river's icy surface. A large white shape appeared from the mist. The car slowly twisted and, with a crunch of metal on wood, its rear smacked into the side of the object.

They had struck a riverboat. Incredulous passengers stared out through the vessel's windows, probably as surprised to see Rhys as he was to see his company car crash into them. The vessel had already come to an abrupt halt in the thick ice, and its captain was hardly going to be on lookout for stray Vauxhall Vectras mid-river.

Rhys caught his breath, and peered at Gwen. 'The insurance claim on this is gonna look pretty bloody unbelievable.'

He could hear screams of terror from the riverboat behind them. Rhys turned in his seat to see why they were yelling. The passengers were wide-eyed, pointing at something beyond the Vectra.

Rhys twisted back, just in time to see a dark mass smash down on the bonnet. The whole car shook with the impact. A slavering head splattered the windscreen with spittle as it bellowed a bestial cry at the occupants of the car. Something like a bulldog, only the size of a Shetland pony, scrabbled to get at them, tearing the wipers and trim off the windscreen. Rhys jerked back in his seat with a bellowing shout of his own, unable to get far enough away from the thing. It was gonna break the window. It was gonna reach in and devour him with those terrible, foam-flecked fangs.

Beside him, in the driver's seat, Gwen released her seatbelt, then shuffled and squirmed. Rhys was terrified that she was going to get out of the car. 'Don't!' he cried. But he didn't know what else to say. He didn't know what to do.

The bulldog monster slammed its head down, and the windshield cracked right across.

Gwen reached forward, double-handed, and pressed a handgun against the glass. That was why she'd removed her seatbelt – to get at her weapon.

She fired twice in rapid succession, a double-tap. The explosive noise of the gun filled the enclosed car. The windshield shattered into fragments. The alien monster's head dissolved in a spray of gore and pus, and the body dropped off the bonnet and disappeared from view.

Gwen burst her door open, dived out, and moved as carefully as she could over the ice to the front of the car. She aimed her weapon, and fired two more bullets into the unseen creature beyond the bonnet.

Rhys sat for a moment and gasped in a desperate breath. His ears still rang with the sound of the first two gunshots. He dropped his chin down on his chest and expelled the air in a shuddering exhalation of relief.

At his feet were the MonstaQuest cards that had scattered out earlier. He scooped them up, straightening them to return them to the glove compartment.

Gwen got back into the car. She was furious, and slammed the heel of her hand against the steering wheel. 'Damn it. Gareth got away.' In the icy cold, her exasperated words formed angry clouds in front of her mouth. 'He abandoned the Mondeo near the opposite bank and hoofed it while I was dealing with that Mahalta.'

Rhys nudged her elbow. 'Did you call it a Mahalta?' He handed her one of the MonstaQuest cards. 'This says it's called an Antebellum.'

'No, the last one we saw, Jack said it was…' Gwen's voice trailed off as she considered the oversized playing card. 'Wait a minute… How can this be on here?'

'That's not the half of it,' continued Rhys. He passed more of the creature cards to her, one by one. A Weevil. A bat-like creature. Something that looked like an angry diplodocus. 'And there are these things called Element Cards, too, see?' He watched her reaction as she studied them. Lightning. Sandstorm. Fog. Ice. 'Too much of a coincidence?' he asked her.

Gwen tapped the cards against her chin as she thought about it.

'Never mind,' said Rhys. 'Fog seems to be clearing a bit now. There's the Stadium, see? Blimey, I've wanted to have a trip down the Taff for ages. Didn't think I'd be doing it in the Vectra, mind.' He considered the icy river. 'D'you think Green Flag will come out this far?'

'I doubt it,' laughed Gwen.

'Told you we should have gone with the RAC.'

'Look over there.' Gwen pointed through the shattered windscreen. She was showing him where Gareth had abandoned his Mondeo.

'I hope that little shit has got third party, because I am gonna sue his arse off.'

'No,' said Gwen. 'I mean it's sinking.'

The Mondeo's rear wheels were slowly vanishing below the surface of the ice.

Gwen's eyes widened. 'That's not good.'

Rhys saw that her breath wasn't clouding in the air any more. Things were warming up, and quickly. The Vectra lurched, and the ice around them crackled and snapped.

They didn't need to discuss it. Both of them wrenched open their doors, and flung themselves out of the car. Rhys could feel the ice beneath his feet turning to slush. Gwen skidded around the car, tottering a little on her heels. She grabbed his hand, and together they half-ran, half-skated their way over to the embankment.

The ice gave way as Rhys jumped for the edge. The river water was still icy cold, and he sank into it up to his waist. The embankment slanted down into the water, and his trainers slid and scraped on the slimy concrete below the water as he tried to prevent himself vanishing beneath the surface.

Gwen wasn't so lucky. The heels of her boots punctured the melting ice, and she plunged right into the river. She surfaced, spluttering at the shock and indignity. Her teeth chattered. Rhys perched on the angled concrete edge, reached out to her, and together they managed to escape the river's freezing embrace.

Only once they had scrambled over the slimy green surface of the concrete and onto the higher, dry area of the embankment did they dare to look back.

The fog had entirely dissipated. The hard white surface of the water had become translucent. In the middle, the riverboat bobbed in the current, now that the river's icy grip had released it. Close to the vessel, the tail end of Rhys's beloved Vectra blurped and bubbled as the car sank into the Taff.

SIXTEEN

Ianto Jones lay on the cold slab of the Torchwood morgue. That much was encouraging, anyway – he hadn't completely lost feeling.

Owen pulled the portable X-ray away from above him. 'You still there, Ianto?'

'Very funny.' Ianto faked a hearty laugh. 'Can I get up yet? This thing is bloody freezing. And so were your hands.'

'What did you expect?' said Owen. 'I blame poor circulation.'

'What?'

'Mine, not yours.'

Ianto sat up, and dangled his legs over the edge of the slab. He peered down at the tiles, and was aware for the first time that this was going to be trickier than he thought. How far up was he? He couldn't see how close to the floor his feet were. 'What's the diagnosis then?'

Owen had stored away his equipment. 'I can't see anything wrong with you.'

'Ho ho,' said Ianto.

'I might get some more from a post-mortem on the other

guy.' Owen indicated the ginger-haired corpse on a stretcher against the wall. The head end was away from Ianto, and he had a gruesome view of a flat cross-section where the visible portion of the dead body suddenly ended, as if it had been guillotined.

'The corpse is half there, half invisible,' explained Owen. 'Should give us some clues.'

'The hospital is gonna want that gurney back,' said Jack. 'Along with the rest of the ambulance.' Toshiko had pushed Jack's wheelchair over to the viewing gallery. Ianto saw them both peering down into the well of the medical area. Even though he was invisible, Ianto felt naked and vulnerable in front of them.

Owen tapped at his analysis computer, and the flat-screen panel beside him resolved itself into a series of scans. 'Hard to do a full physical examination,' he admitted, and waved his bandaged hand at the display. 'Easy enough to confirm that vital signs are OK. Nothing unusual with your blood pressure or resps, Ianto. But fluids analysis is a bit tricky, 'cause I can't see it to test it. Or in the case of blood, I can't take a sample. So the reference ranges on these charts are meaningless.'

'We can tell that you're literally invisible in the optical spectrum,' noted Toshiko. She walked down the short flight of steps, and pointed at the display. 'Actually, as far down as ultraviolet at one end and up through thermal infrared at the other. Wavelengths in air between about two hundred and eleven hundred nanometers.'

'Mind you…' Owen tapped another control, and the image changed. 'I was able to take X-rays. You've got no broken bones. And the best I can tell from the ultrasound scan is that you have no serious disruption to your internal organs. So while this is an unusually severe and persistent injury, it doesn't look like it'll be fatal. In A&E, I'd probably send you back to your GP...' He stifled a laugh. 'Except he probably wouldn't be able to see you for ages.'

Ianto's exasperated groan filled the room. He knew this was Owen's revenge for all the 'dead' jokes Ianto had been using on him.

'I'm so hungry,' Ianto's voice shivered. 'But maybe I'll freeze to death first.'

'Oh yeah. Tosh wants to analyse your invisible clothes,' agreed Owen. He indicated the empty slab to Jack. 'He had to take them off anyway, 'cause they were covered in tiger shit.'

'Wait a minute...' Jack cocked a saucy eyebrow. 'Am I hearing this correctly? Ianto is sitting there... naked?'

'Like, but unlike, one of my recurring nightmares,' said Ianto's voice in a plaintive tone.

Jack stared at the ceiling and laughed aloud. 'Oh, that is *such* an unfair advantage in naked hide-and-seek...' He trailed off as he realised Owen and Toshiko were both looking at him. 'What?'

Owen shook his head sorrowfully. '*So* don't want to know,' he told Jack.

'It's a bit... creepy having you walk around the place like that,' Toshiko said.

'I kinda like it,' said Jack.

'He's naked.'

'You say that like it's a bad thing.'

'Here's an idea,' suggested Owen. 'I could bandage your head. Like the invisible man. I'm good with bandages. Medical doctor, trained and everything.'

Ianto was unimpressed. 'I'd prefer a cure.'

'Not sure there is one,' Owen confessed. 'We haven't even

got the device that did this. Your Achenbrite mates must have taken it with them.'

This piqued Jack's interest, and he leaned on the rail to call down to Toshiko. 'Any information on Achenbrite yet?'

'It's collating now.'

'OK, patch it through to the Boardroom. We're about to start.'

Toshiko pointed at his wheelchair. 'Do you want a push?'

Jack seized the chair's wide wheels in his strong hands. 'Give me a head start. See you in five minutes.'

'See ya,' grinned Owen.

Ianto sighed so heavily that papers moved on the work surface beside him. 'Am I going to stay like this?'

Owen cocked his head as though contemplating this calamity. 'May depend on new cell growth. Difficult to test anything on that dead guy.'

'I thought that nails and hair grew after death?'

Owen stroked his own clean-shaven chin. 'Take it from an expert, that's a myth. Best you can hope for is that your cells renew visibly as they get replaced. We'll only know that by waiting.' He was fighting not to smile again. 'You should keep a record of what you notice. Maybe some regular entries in your diary, Ianto.' The smile couldn't be suppressed any longer. 'You could write it in invisible ink.'

'We're out of invisible ink,' said Toshiko immediately.

'How can you tell?' Owen responded.

Toshiko and Owen giggled like kids.

Ianto said, 'I am still here, you know.'

Owen smirked. 'If you're blushing, mate, no one can tell.' He pondered the empty space where he thought Ianto was.

'I'll see you in the Boardroom,' snapped Ianto. 'Even if you won't see me.'

He jumped down onto the freezing cold mortuary floor and stalked away to the sound of Owen and Toshiko's laughter.

Gwen sat at the Boardroom table while she waited for everyone to gather. She turned over the few MonstaQuest cards from Rhys's pack that hadn't floated off downriver. They had dried out, but were crinkled and discoloured, and they smelled a bit, too. She sniffed her own fingers surreptitiously. Even after a thorough shower, she wasn't convinced she'd entirely washed away the dank stench of the River Taff. Toshiko would be the first person to notice that, but Toshiko would also be the last person who'd ever want to tell her.

When Toshiko came in, she was fiddling with some bit of alien tech she'd retrieved from the Vaults. As soon as she was seated, she began to tap notes into the table-top computer in preparation for the meeting. The tech was like a squarish PDA with undulating edges, and it sat on the velvet bag from which she'd taken it.

'You OK?' Gwen asked her. 'Owen check you over after your concussion?'

'Yeah. Yes.' Fussing made Toshiko embarrassed. 'How's Rhys?'

Gwen laughed. 'Gone home for a hot bath.' She smiled at the thought of him dripping his way through the November streets, drawing curious looks from passers-by. Just as she had, until she'd found the blessed anonymity of Torchwood's invisible elevator in Millennium Square. 'Under the circumstances, I decided it was only fair to let him go to the match later.' She sniffed her fingers again. 'What's keeping the others?'

Toshiko grimaced. 'They were a bit upset about the mess around their desks.'

'Not your fault.'

'You know how house-proud Ianto is. I hardly dare drop biscuit crumbs.'

'Still, you've got a new friend,' added Gwen.

'Yes,' agreed Toshiko. 'I think I could grow to like that pteranodon after all.'

'I *hate* the damn thing,' said Ianto's voice from nowhere, yet nearby.

Toshiko startled, and put her hand to her mouth. The chair next to her at the table shifted sideways a little.

'Well, you're not the one who has to clear up all the pteranodon crap,' said Ianto. 'And what do you mean, "house-proud"?'

Toshiko's face flushed. She put her hand down again, and tried to sit a little straighter in her chair as she recomposed herself. 'I'm sorry, Ianto. I forgot you were here.'

Ianto sighed noisily. 'Time was that I didn't need to be invisible for that to happen.'

The Boardroom door slid aside. Jack breezed in, propelling his wheelchair with powerful movements. His lap was full of equipment, papers, and assorted objects rescued from the Hub's main chamber. When he bumped into the edge of the desk, items clattered down onto its polished surface.

'Quite a mess,' he grinned. 'We rescued some bits for the meeting. Couple of unbroken PDAs. Notepads that didn't get covered in dino-blood.'

'I'd just cleaned that floor,' Ianto said. 'You could have eaten off it.' There was a distinctive sound that Gwen eventually worked out was Ianto's stomach rumbling. 'I could murder a meat feast.'

'It will not look pretty when you chew it,' Owen said. 'And it will look disgusting when you're digesting it.'

'So I'm going to starve to death, am I?' Ianto asked defiantly.

Owen tutted. 'You're not going to look pretty if your new cells do become visible.

Jack patted thin air. Gwen wasn't even sure if Ianto's head was under the hand, or whether he was kidding around. 'OK, I've changed my mind,' announced Jack. 'Ianto, go get some clothes on. Don't wanna see your organs walking around the Hub like a bag of giblets.'

The empty chair pushed back. 'So I should go and get dressed now?'

Owen had a wide, pleased grin on his face. 'Who said you couldn't in the first place?'

'OK, let's review what we've got so far.' Jack picked up a pack of MonstaQuest cards. 'Multiple alien incursions, all described on these illustrated cards.' He placed the pack on the desk like he was playing a strange game of solitaire. 'Weevil in the church of Holy Innocents. Another Weevil attacking a bus full of people.'

Toshiko indicated another card in Jack's collection. 'That one there, the bat-creature. That was at the shopping centre.'

'Ooh, nasty,' said Jack. 'That's a Kiroptan. An omnivore. Lots of teeth, little discrimination.'

Gwen pushed forward the tattered cards she had retrieved from the river. 'Mahalta. Attacked Rhys's car. No, no,' she waved away Jack's concern. 'He's OK.'

'These names are wrong,' Owen observed. 'That one says "Antebellum", not Mahalta. That Weevil claims to be a

"Toothsome".'

'Someone's created these without knowing what they are,' said Jack.

'Gareth Portland. Printed them up from his home workshop in Rhiwbina.'

'Classy,' smiled Jack.

'Now out of action,' continued Gwen, 'after that convenient fire. Killed his girlfriend and his business at the same time.'

Jack shifted some of the cards around the desk before him. 'But do these things *reflect* reality, or do they *cause* it?'

'There's something else,' Gwen said. She presented several more MonstaQuest illustrations. 'Element cards. Rain, Snow, Fog, Lightning… Inexplicable real events that we've seen in the last twenty-four hours.'

Toshiko punched up a new display on the flat-screen. 'Spikes of Rift activity correspond to all these locations in that time period. It's rare to have so many localised peaks of such intensity. One big burst you could understand, plus the usual background leakages. But these are extraordinary. And they map to the freak meteorological manifestations Gwen mentioned.'

Owen frowned. 'What about the Brakkanee at the zoo? No freak weather. No card. Just coincidence?'

'I saw one of those cards in the tiger enclosure,' said Ianto's voice in the doorway.

They all turned to look.

'And the whole place was sodden,' continued Ianto. 'I heard the keepers talking about a crazy downpour that happened when one of their keepers was killed…' His voice dropped as he must have seen they were all gaping.

Gwen coughed and apologised. 'Sorry, Ianto, it's just…'

'It's just you don't expect to see a suit walking around

on its own.' Ianto's voice came from just above the neatly knotted tie that encircled the neckline of an empty, maroon-coloured shirt. Give him credit, thought Gwen, he'd made an effort.

The suit pulled out a chair, sat on it, shot the cuffs of its shirt, and placed its sleeves on the desk. 'So, these cards. Too much of a coincidence, wouldn't you say?' The sleeves seemed to draw Jack's pack of MonstaQuest cards across the desk and started to riffle through them in mid air.

Toshiko was displaying more screens of analysis. Gwen's heart sank a little. Toshiko loved her histograms and her pie charts, but sometimes it was like she was lost in the detail and missing the obvious. After listening to her explain the statistics, Gwen interrupted: 'So, what you're saying is that there's been an increase in alien incursions around Cardiff, but that the Weevil attacks have increased most of all. Even in places where we didn't get them before?'

'Yes,' admitted Toshiko, sounding a bit disappointed to have her analysis so comprehensively summarised. 'I've done a deep-dive analysis of the available data. Looked for a possible further link. And I think I found one. Remember this?' She indicated the alien tech on the table. 'It was unearthed in the archaeological dig around the motte at Twmpath.'

The device lay on its soft velvet cover. The closer Gwen looked at it, the more the velvet appeared iridescent under the Boardroom lights. Like the lining of a coat her mum used to have. Toshiko cupped the device in her hands and closed her eyes.

'The usual question, then,' Owen said. 'What is that?'

Toshiko raised her hands, like a votive offering. 'It's a kind of catalogue.' The image on the wall-hanging flat-screen smoothly transitioned into a matrix of alien glyphs and images.

'Monster hotline?' sniggered Owen.

'Two large Weevils, please. Make one of them extra spiky,' Ianto suggested.

The image flickered. 'Be nice to me,' said Toshiko quietly. 'It's controlled by strong emotions.'

'Er… find your happy place, Tosh,' suggested Jack quietly. 'Put them on the screen, and not on the table.'

Toshiko concentrated. The illustrations on the flat-screen whirled and rearranged themselves. 'Recognise these?'

'Hey, the gang's all here,' said Jack. 'Kiroptan, Mahalta, Weevil… ooh, Hoix and Vondrax too, I see. All our boys, and some others to make up numbers.'

The image flickered back to the original display when Toshiko opened her eyes. She lowered the device to the desk. 'Twmpath Castle is on the northern edge of Rhiwbina. Isn't that where you said Gareth Portland lived?'

Gwen nodded. 'Maybe Gareth has a device just like that. Used it as the basis for these cards he's been creating?'

'Interesting,' said Ianto. He'd been shuffling the scattered MonstaQuest pack around on the table. Now the cards were sorted into neat piles. Typical Ianto, thought Gwen. 'There are more Weevils in this pack than all the other creatures put together.'

Gwen had a thought: 'Like pawns in chess?'

'There are thousands of other creatures listed in this catalogue.' Toshiko held up the squarish device, and its curved edges caught the light in the Boardroom. 'A whole menagerie. We could barely cope if just one of each kind came through.'

'An alien zoo,' said Ianto.

'With the gates wide open,' snapped Jack. 'The predators are escaping. And in Gareth's hands, they've got a season ticket to Cardiff.'

Owen sounded less convinced. 'C'mon! This is just one guy toying with us, isn't it? We find him, give him a smack, and confiscate it. He's stumbled on this bit of tech, found he got more than he bargained for.'

'Could that explain all these?' Toshiko had stood up to point at the flat-screen. It showed her original analysis of unexplained deaths across South Wales. 'The device may bring the creatures through the Rift. But each set of MonstaQuest cards is like a tarot pack. They focus the mind of anyone near a Rift fault line who is enthusiastic, creative, or highly emotional.'

Gwen recalled the games shop owner, and how he'd unwittingly conjured up a fire creature. 'And when it appears?'

'The victims reinforce it,' said Toshiko. 'Their surprise or horror makes the manifestation corporeal. And deadly.'

'Like those people on the bus,' recalled Owen. He looked more worried now.

'It can't be just one guy.' Jack stared at each of them in turn.

Gwen recognised it as the way he commanded their attention, got their respect. Through the urgency of his words and the fierce passion in his eyes when he looked at you, looked into you. Or, in Ianto's case at the moment, through you. Gwen saw Jack's gaze falter as it reached the empty suit. Was that confusion or tenderness? Maybe a bit of both.

'Achenbrite are involved in this, too. They must be. Their operatives disrupted our comms at the mall and during the bus attack. They were on the scene at both the mall and the zoo. And it was their device that injured Ianto.' He pushed his wheelchair back from the desk. 'We reconvene here in half an hour. Gimme information, and gimme options.'

Jack was on crutches when they got back to the Boardroom. The metal sticks were propped against his chair. He had his damaged foot up on the desk, and was perusing it with the curiosity of a kid examining a scabby knee. Gwen winced when she saw the savage scoring in the skin of his lower leg. His foot still seemed to be attached only by chunks of raw flesh, like hammered steak.

He lifted the leg back below the desk. 'Sorry.'

'You must get used to it.'

'Never do,' he said. He tested his forehead with an exploratory finger, and checked his reflection in the shiny surface of the desk.

Jack settled himself into his seat between Owen and Toshiko. On the opposite side of the desk, Ianto's suit made itself comfortable in the chair next to Gwen. The suit had brought a plate of freshly made sandwiches on wholemeal bread. 'My special tuna mix,' he murmured to Gwen.

Across the table, Jack was ready for the meeting to start. 'All right. Tell me about Achenbrite.'

Toshiko sat up a little straighter in her chair, if that were possible. 'Achenbrite is a shell company that sprang into new life over the past year. Someone's done a good job erasing records and back-ups from Companies House. I did manage to pull a few details through a back door in the Compliance Unit in Natgarw, because one of the investing companies received a late-filing penalty. Parker Plastics, registered in Plas Hendre, and owned by the late Henry John Parker. Better known to us when he was alive as an enthusiastic collector of alien ephemera.'

'That's telling,' mused Jack. 'And now?'

'No evidence of it manufacturing anything, nor providing services. Not enough history for tracing payroll through HMRC – no VAT, nor NI, no Income or Corporation Tax. They don't even appear in Yellow Pages.'

Jack clutched his face in mock horror.

Toshiko tapped up the details on the flat-screen. A warehouse complex rotated on the display, a three-dimensional rendering in blue wireframe. Key areas were labelled or highlighted with brighter spots in the image. A translation key filled the lower left of the screen.

'The Achenbrite facility is a single-storey unit,' Toshiko explained. 'Built on a place where there was significant Rift activity in previous years.'

Ianto snorted. 'Where isn't, these days?' The suit of his sleeve was reaching out to the plate of sandwiches, but Toshiko slapped his hand away.

'Difference is, now there is nothing.'

'That's not very likely.' Jack frowned at the display as though this would disprove it. 'There's always some Rift trace around anything in Cardiff.'

'Like background radiation,' agreed Toshiko. 'You could understand it might quiesce...'

'Quiesce?' interrupted Jack. 'Is that even a word, Tosh?'

'All right, fade away to nothing. Vanish. The complete absence of it makes the factory stick out like a sore thumb. Usually I look for evidence of raised energy levels, not gaps in the field.' Toshiko flipped the display to an aerial shot of the Achenbrite offices. Three intersecting circles displayed over the top of it, like a Venn diagram. 'Too regular to be accidental. They're concealing themselves from detection.'

'Too perfectly,' noted Jack. 'What else?'

'All the other conventional evidence suggests that it's empty. It has no apparent power requirements because it's not connected to the National Grid, and yet you see that there are lights on. So someone's home. I hacked the Royal Mail, and there's nothing there either. What kind of business has no post in or out?'

'Maybe they hate the taste of glue,' suggested Owen. 'Or they do everything electronically?'

'No phones,' revealed Toshiko. 'No landlines, no cell signal. But there's visible activity on-site. Including a daily visit by their MD.' She displayed a blurred photograph of a woman with long, steel-grey hair. 'Jennifer Portland.'

'Have we heard of her?' asked Gwen.

Toshiko shook her head. 'No. But you've met her son.' Another grainy picture appeared. A lank-haired young man with high cheekbones. 'Remember Gareth?'

'All right!' Jack had that evangelical look of determination in his eyes now. 'Now we've connected the guy who's bringing these creatures through the Rift to the people who have recaptured at least two of them. We need to know what's in that Achenbrite facility.'

'On the case,' said Toshiko. 'I've already got into their external-access systems. But everything else in there – cameras, communications, business processes – they're all on a separate, completely isolated server. Someone has to go in.'

'They were able to disrupt our comms,' said Ianto, reaching for a sandwich.

Toshiko slapped his invisible hand away again, and slid the plate away. 'So it has to be a personal visit. You seem like

170

the ideal candidate.'

'Riiight!' grinned Jack. 'Unless you've eaten something, Ianto, because then you'd look like a floating mass of half-digested... what are those?'

'Ianto's Special,' said Gwen.

'I know that,' said Jack. 'But what's in the sandwiches?'

'Can't I even have *one*?' bleated Ianto. He pondered what Toshiko was suggesting. 'Wait a minute. You're suggesting that I walk into that place naked?'

'I can get you into the building,' Toshiko explained. 'Owen just spent his lunchtime dropping computer memory sticks in the Achenbrite car park, and near their entrance doors. Places where they might plausibly have fallen out of people's pockets. Several staff members came back after lunch and found them. And two people inserted them into their office machines to look for pictures or files that might give them a clue about who owned them.'

Jack was impressed. 'I'm glad you're on *our* side.'

'Of course, they didn't spot the key-logging software that was automatically being installed on their machines,' explained Toshiko, clearly pleased with the success of her ruse. 'So I've also captured all their most valuable passwords and cracked their badge access. So while I can't access their server, I have all the information you'll need to do that when you're on-site.'

'Get yer kit off, Ianto,' crowed Owen delightedly. 'You're going in! Tosh has programmed you into their access system under a false identity. We chose it from our porn names.'

'Now I'm intrigued,' said Jack.

'Name of your first pet plus the name of the street you grew up in,' Owen continued. 'I had a dog called Bobby and grew up in Warren Drive, so I'm Bobby Warren. Gwen is Tiggi

Locke. And Ianto,' he concluded with a note of incredulity, 'is Trevor Swanson.'

Jack roared with laughter.

'Who the hell calls their pet dog Trevor?' spluttered Gwen.

Toshiko took a dainty bite from a tuna sandwich in a futile effort to hide her amusement.

'Come on, Trevor,' said Jack. 'Time you were going.'

The suit of clothes started to remove its jacket and tie at the desk. Ianto's sullen reaction was evident through his body language alone.

SEVENTEEN

Jack said it would be funny to have Ianto drive the SUV to Achenbrite. 'No, hear me out – the bandages, the sunglasses, the whole Claude Raines shtick.'

'Too bizarre,' Gwen told him.

'Hey, a dead guy drove us to the Pharm—' Jack began, but Gwen cut him off.

'Ianto, you're in the back, I'm up front, Owen you can drive. And you…' She turned to Jack, still hobbling about on his crutches. 'You stay right here with Tosh.'

'Who died and made you Captain?' complained Jack in a surly tone.

Gwen snatched a crutch off him and carried it away from his office and across to the lift platform. 'Come and get it, boss.'

Jack didn't even get as far as the walkway over the pool. He lurched against the rail, gasping and grimacing with pain.

Gwen propped the crutch against the base of the stainless steel tower for him to collect in his own time. She activated the exit lift, which began its ascent to Roald Dahl Plass. As it rose, she balanced by holding on to Ianto's hairy, invisible forearm like some odd mime act. She could hear Ianto chuckling. Jack's outraged expression grew smaller.

'We know that Achenbrite can block our comms,' Jack shouted up at them. 'But we don't know whether they can intercept them. If we're adopting radio silence for this mission, I don't want to be stuck here with Tosh.'

'Thanks, Jack,' Toshiko called from her workstation.

'No offence, Tosh. I'll just be kicking my heels.'

Toshiko pouted at him as she waved farewell to Gwen. 'Well, your heel, anyway.'

A faint sheen of fine, clinging rain wafted off the Bay and across the Plass as Gwen and Ianto made their way to where Owen was to deliver the SUV. The rain meant there were fewer pedestrians to avoid, but it was still odd to hear the slapping sound of Ianto's bare feet on the wooden boards.

Under the cover of the bus shelter, Gwen could make out the faint outline of Ianto's head, shoulders and back from the fine covering of rainwater. A tell-tale patina of his whereabouts. She got him to stand still for a moment and, for want of anything else, slipped off her jacket and wiped his back with the lining. The cold November air chilled her to goose bumps. Gwen could feel Ianto shivering.

'You poor thing,' she said. When Owen drew up in the SUV, she banged on the driver's window and urged him to crank the heating up. 'We'll try to park as close as possible to the Achenbrite place without drawing attention to ourselves,' she told Ianto. 'No point getting you any more frozen than absolutely necessary.'

The rear door of the SUV opened and closed by itself.

Gwen slipped into the passenger seat and buckled up.

'Knowing that Owen is driving,' said Ianto's voice from behind her, 'that's a very wise precaution.'

Gwen laughed softly as she remembered what Rhys had said that same morning. 'The difference between knowledge and wisdom. That's one of Jack's, isn't it?'

'Something to do with tomatoes?' Ianto asked. 'Yes, that'll be one of Jack's. Sounds more profound than it is, so he uses it when he's trying to con you.' He buckled himself incongruously into the seatbelt. 'Ask me in an hour whether walking into the enemy camp naked was a wise decision.'

On the fourth attempt, Jack managed to get across the Hub without his crutch. He traversed the route from his office, across behind the water tower, and then over the walkway. The throbbing in his damaged leg was intense, but the satisfaction of completing the route was even greater. He approached Toshiko's workstation, and thought he heard her say to herself: 'I hope I did good.' Or maybe it was 'You did good.'

Well, yeah, he had done good, and he deserved a reward for his efforts. So he helped himself to the jar of candy on Toshiko's desk. Toshiko started, and even gave a little squeal of shock. But she recovered her composure quickly enough to minimise the window of the application she'd been working on.

'What was that?' asked Jack.

She blanched. 'Research,' she said after a beat. She tugged the jar from his hand. 'Hey, Gwen bought those bon-bons for me!'

Jack held one between his finger and thumb, and waggled it provocatively.

'The jar spilled,' Toshiko warned him. 'I had to retrieve three or four of them from the filthy dirty floor.'

Jack looked at the bon-bon, and considered the size of the

jar. 'I like those odds,' he decided, and popped the candy in his mouth. He pointed to the stuffed plush toy on her desk. 'What's that for?'

Toshiko smiled her secret smile. 'It's for when Owen comes to ask me a question for the fifth time each day about how to fix his computer. The sort of thing he should be able to work out for himself. So I insist that he asks this stuffed tiger before he interrupts me.'

He raised his eyebrows at her. 'Does it work?'

Toshiko scratched the tiger affectionately between its velour ears. 'It has an eighty per cent success rate.'

Jack chuckled, and drew a chair up next to her. 'Not as good as you,' he said. 'This computer of ours, Tosh. Organic, living, intuitive technology light years ahead of anything on Earth. But you got it as soon as you used it. No one understands it like you do, Tosh. What would we do without you?'

'I thought about that today,' she said quietly. Her fingers tapped nervously on her mouse, and the pointer on her display screen jiggled in response.

'The sauropod that got in here?' Jack asked. 'Yeah, that must have been a close thing. But you know what? You did good.'

She gave him a sharp look.

'I mean it,' he smiled. 'I take all the credit, of course,' he added grandly, 'I only pick the best. So, watcha doin'?'

Toshiko didn't look at him. Instead of answering his question, she pointed to the stuffed tiger. Jack laughed good-naturedly, and Toshiko joined in.

'I'm connecting the dots,' she told him eventually. 'I'm doing some conventional data mining. It's the online version of Ianto snooping naked around Achenbrite, but it's less likely to arouse suspicion.'

Jack smiled. 'Ianto snooping while naked. That's arousing, right there.'

Toshiko opened a load of web browser windows, and manipulated them so they displayed across all the available flat-screen display space above her desk. News reports, NHS records, Police SOC reports, birth certificates. They were all linked by dynamically moving lines. And at the centre was a photograph of a young man with sharp cheekbones. Startling green eyes stared out from beneath greasy centre-parted hair.

'Gareth Portland,' said Jack. 'Those lines make him look like the spider at the centre of a web.'

'He's the connection that binds all these facts and events,' agreed Toshiko. 'Freak meteorological events, MonstaQuest franchises, family addresses, that sort of thing. There's a psych report for when he was treated for anger management as a teenager. But it's the sudden deaths that interest me.'

'Never say that in a public place,' Jack joked. Toshiko peered over her spectacles at him. 'Sorry, go on, Tosh.'

'The priest you found this morning? Gareth was one of his altar boys at Holy Innocents. This young woman here? She was the school pupil who he fought with in Year 10 and got a two-month suspension. This couple here are his former neighbours. The zookeeper who got killed? He supervised Gareth's work placement. Gareth had a MonstaQuest franchise at Pendefig Mall – and that burned down this morning. Gareth's girlfriend died in a house fire at his home. And there's more.'

Jack clucked his tongue. 'That's either one *really* unlucky guy, or...'

'... he is the spider at the heart of the web.' Toshiko lifted her plush tiger, and Jack now saw that it had been sat on the alien 'zoo catalogue' device. 'He's got one of these,' Toshiko continued. 'A device that takes advantage of Gareth's fragile emotions by getting him worked up about all sorts of things. He thinks that he's exploiting it, Jack. But I think it's using him.'

Jack turned the catalogue device over in his hand. 'Better find him, Tosh.'

'Is he in the Achenbrite facility?'

'I don't think so,' said Jack. 'But remember you said you found that place when you worked out what it *wasn't* showing us?'

'Sure.'

'Look for catastrophes or deaths that *could* have happened but *didn't*, or haven't yet. Dive deeper into your data, Tosh. That's how you'll find him.'

Toshiko moved her hands to her keyboard. 'And what about Ianto?' she asked.

'No way to contact him now. He's on his own.' He saw that Toshiko had stopped typing, and was looking at him worriedly. 'Don't worry,' he told her. 'I picked the best, remember?'

But he hoped his voice didn't betray his true fears.

EIGHTEEN

Ianto unclipped his seatbelt as the SUV slowed to a halt. He worked out that it was easier to use the muscle memory of unlatching it than to look for the belt buckle. It was too disorienting to work out where his invisible fingers were in relation to the things he was trying to manipulate.

Owen parked the SUV behind the For Sale hoarding that hid a defunct print company from the main swag of the industrial estate. This meant they wouldn't draw attention to themselves by parking right in the Achenbrite car park. But it would also require Ianto to pad barefoot over an access road and across the car park.

Toshiko's voice filtered through the SUV's speaker phone. 'You'll be out of radio contact, Ianto,' she explained.

'I appreciate that,' he murmured. 'No earcomms.'

Owen laughed. 'That'd be a giveaway. Not much point being invisible if whatever's stuck in your ear floats around in mid air.'

They'd decided that even the 'virtual contact' lenses could draw attention, in the way a couple of flies might catch the eye of an observer. So Ianto was going in to Achenbrite literally naked. No clothes, no comms, and no weapon.

'Well, anyway, you'll have to memorise a sixteen-number access code,' continued Toshiko. 'So I made it 2738-4947-3354-9937.'

Ianto started to groan halfway through the numbers.

Gwen sucked air through her teeth. 'Yeah, Tosh. How's he ever going to remember that?'

'He can use the alphanumeric keypad to type in the corresponding letters from the start of a memorable phrase.' Toshiko's voice sounded pleased. Ianto imagined she was doing that little 'aha' smile that Jack seemed to find so adorable, the one that meant she knew she'd been especially clever. 'The phrase I've chosen is *Creu Gwir fel Gwydr o Ffwrnais Awen.*'

Ianto should have guessed. 'Very funny,' he said, though he didn't feel amused.

'Ohhh,' said Gwen. 'That bit of poetry on the front of the Millennium Centre.'

'Exactly,' said Toshiko. 'I thought I should choose something you see every day, Ianto.'

Ianto threw open the rear door of the SUV. 'You'll be sorry,' he called back into the vehicle. 'You know that, Tosh, don't you?'

'What does he mean?' Gwen asked.

Toshiko giggled, said she'd explain later, and ended the call. Ianto slammed the door and slunk away.

None of the adjacent business units seemed to be busy, so there was no one to hear Ianto's curses and sharp cries of pain as he traversed the roughly pitted surface of the roadway.

He kept to the side of the route up to the Achenbrite building, and avoided the sharp gravel by treading on the path's edging to spare his feet. The icy cold concrete of the border froze his soles. Low branches snagged in the hairs on Ianto's legs as he balanced. Their thorns scratched his skin, maybe even drawing blood, though how would he be able to tell?

The original plan was for him to tailgate into the building immediately after one of the Achenbrite employees. After hopping from foot to foot in the cold air for ten minutes, he could tell that was never going to work. No one appeared to be entering or leaving the building. Where had everyone gone? Owen had reported the place was buzzing with activity earlier when he'd dropped the memory sticks. Yet now it was mid-afternoon on a busy Saturday, and it might as well have been Sunday for all the activity around the place. Impossible to tell what was happening inside the building, either, because even the main reception had opaque glass windows.

So it was time for Plan B, which was to use the access authority that Toshiko had remotely programmed into the Achenbrite security system.

Ianto raised his hand to the reception door, to shade it as he peered through. He stifled a laugh at the absurdity of attempting this with invisible hands. He resorted instead to squinting through the door, noting with curiosity how his invisible breath condensed and became visible on the smoked glass.

The main area and front desk were deserted. He turned his attention to the proximity badge reader at chest height by the door. It had a recessed display screen, with a keypad for anyone who needed to get conventional access without an ID card.

He tapped in the sixteen numbers and waited. Of course that number was something he saw every day – it was identical to his supposedly secret Torchwood login code. And he'd chosen it for exactly the reason that Toshiko had just explained to Gwen. She was giving him a coded message that he would understand but Gwen and Owen would not: sneakily telling Ianto that she had cracked his personal login.

The door buzzed open, and Ianto slipped swiftly inside. The only risk was if any security camera saw the door move on its own.

The warmth of the entrance area and the soft texture of its carpet tiles were a welcome change. A couple of CCTV cameras poked out of the wall as visible deterrents to intruders, but it was evident from their stillness and extinguished indicator lights that they were not operational. That was odd.

The main desk was still unoccupied. When he checked behind it, Ianto found papers scattered across the desk and on the floor by the overturned chair. It was as though the receptionist had rushed away somewhere. They'd left their display monitor unlocked, too, so Ianto had a look at the information on that.

One side of the screen displayed the name Trevor Swanson, because that was the alias Toshiko had specified in the system to allow coded entry. He smiled at the picture she'd chosen to accompany it: a photo of Barry Nelson, who had once played James Bond on TV. Toshiko knew Ianto's enthusiasms, as well as his password.

He stopped smiling when he saw what was being cross-referenced on the other side of the screen. Names and faces scrolled upwards: Douglas Caldwell, Gerald Carter, Lydia Childs, Gwen Cooper, Suzie Costello, Harriet Derbyshire...

A list of former and current Torchwood operatives in

Cardiff. How the hell could Achenbrite know about them?

Ianto stared around the reception as though, impossibly, he might be observed. There was no one there, and the CCTV was dead. Yet more than ever he felt his own vulnerability as he stood by the all-too knowing screen, naked and defenceless.

He keyed in his access code at the next proximity badge reader, and slipped through into a linking corridor.

There were two further doors to either side, and another one ten metres away at the far end. A fluorescent tube sputtered behind a transparent ceiling panel. Halfway down, above head height, was another pair of CCTV cameras, but their lights were dead. By the time Ianto had walked far enough to examine the cameras, the carpet tiles felt gritty under his bare feet.

Ianto hunkered down to check, and discovered a scattering of fine sand. Some of it had drifted up against the skirting. It built into a higher, heaped pile against the far door. Rooted in the sand, fitfully illuminated by the overhead light, a row of four thin-stemmed double-headed flowers nodded in the breeze.

Wait a minute… what breeze?

He shuffled away from them, his feet scuffing sand. The flowers twisted their heads around to face him. Ianto sprang high into the air and away. The petals on the double-headed blooms snapped open, and a shower of seeds spurted onto the spot where Ianto had been standing only moments earlier. Some of the scattered seeds struck the wallpaper just above the skirting, where they stuck and quivered like little darts.

Ianto scrabbled to locate the nearest handle, then wrenched the door open. It was a meeting room, and it was in darkness. He slapped at the adjacent wall, finding the switches by touch. As the lights pinked and fluttered into life, he hurried into the room.

The dismembered bodies of half a dozen Achenbrite staff had been discarded across the meeting room. They slumped against the wall or over the table in the centre. In some cases, their limbs had been ripped off, ragged flesh the only visible remains in grey uniforms darkened with purple blood. Further smears of blood and savage indentations in the plaster walls bore witness to a fight with some huge creature.

Two corpses were decapitated. The eyes of the others were wide, the faces twisted at the final sight of some unknown horror. An undulating surface of sand half-buried the furthest bodies, like the ripples on a beach at low tide. Against the far wall were more of the double-headed flowers, though these had collapsed in limp rows. He could see where their seeds had sprayed over the dead bodies and taken root.

The dead men had been caught in the middle of a poker game. None of them were holding their weapons, which were still racked against the wall. A conventional set of playing cards, along with pound coins and fivers, were scattered across the table. But Ianto saw other, larger cards on the table – brightly coloured MonstaQuest images of deadly creatures. He recognised the one named 'Bludgeon Beast' as a Hoix, but the 'Destructor' and the 'Janbri Warrior' were new to him. The fourth one simply said 'Sandstorm'.

Ianto discovered that he had backed himself against the wall, as though desperate to get as far away as possible from this carnage. He sidled along it, aiming for the exit door again, and his foot caught on a dismembered arm. Its hand clutched at a PDA-device. Ianto recognised it – some of the

Achenbrite staff he'd seen at the zoo had been using them.

Wincing with distaste, Ianto recovered the PDA and studied the screen. It showed the image of a surveillance suite with banks of monitors. It had the same décor as this meeting room, including the blood smears up the wall. The blurred image was from a CCTV camera high up on a wall. In the centre of the room it showed the piled bodies of the MonstaQuest creatures, and another dead Achenbrite man.

Ianto reversed out of the meeting room. He skirted the wall carefully to avoid the spitting flowers, traversed the corridor, and tried the opposite door.

This led into a conference room, and a real contrast to what he'd seen elsewhere. The overhead lighting revealed that everything was in its place, undamaged. A wide table with a polished walnut top dominated the space. It had an in-built keyboard, and two speaker phones with satellite microphones sat at its centre. One wall was a huge display screen made up of sixteen large flat-screen monitors. A sign opposite identified a 'Monitor Room'.

Ianto's feet sank right into the plush carpet as he made his way over to the door. Through the window in it he could see the surveillance gear that the PDA had shown him, the mashed remains of an Achenbrite security guard, and the clumsy pile of dead monsters. His hand was on the door when a commotion from behind him was accompanied by a shouted warning.

'Get away from that door!'

Ianto whirled on his heel. In the frame of the opposite doorway stood a thin-faced, middle-aged woman in a well-cut business suit. Her trim copper hair starkly outlined her head, though the effect was spoiled by the gas mask that covered her face. Angry eyes peered out at him through the top of the mask. The woman wasn't armed. Both hands were occupied holding a flat black rectangle, like she was carrying a box of chocolates.

Behind her, two Achenbrite guards in grey boiler suits and gas masks were using long-handled sprays to soak the outer corridor. Ianto could swear that the plants were making high-pitched squealing sounds.

'Get away from the door,' repeated the woman, her voice metallic through the mask's speaker. 'Please.'

He hadn't touched the door handle. How could she tell he was there? He hadn't left any footprints on the carpet. But he was still holding the Achenbrite PDA.

He stepped to the left of the door, but at the same time tossed the PDA in a shallow arc to the right. It bounced and scraped across the conference table. Ianto stopped by an open cupboard full of stationery, and held his breath.

The woman's eyes had followed the PDA as it came to rest against one of the conference phones. When she looked back again, she didn't stare at the Monitor Room door, but directly to where Ianto had moved.

'Thank you.' She set the chocolate box down on the conference table. With her hands free, she could peel the gas mask backwards over her head. She shook her copper hair straight again, and returned her gaze to where Ianto was still trying to hold his breath. She looked straight into his eyes. When she spoke again, her voice was calm, and slightly amused. 'We had to asphyxiate those creatures in there. The gas has not dispersed, and it's highly toxic to humans.' She set down the gas mask, and retrieved the flat box. 'Come in, boys,' she called over her shoulder. 'No need for your masks.'

The two Achenbrite guards stepped into the conference

room, their gas masks clipped to their belts. They flanked the woman, each taller than her by a head. Ianto could see a family resemblance in their eyes, and in their coppery red hair.

'Thank you, boys,' said the woman. 'I thought you should meet Mr Jones, who has decided to make an appearance.'

Ianto muffled a gasp. She knew his name. And she knew where he was.

The woman tapped some recessed controls on the chocolate box. A wide angle of pale lilac light shot across the room in a two-second flash. Ianto blinked involuntarily as it dazzled him. When he opened his eyes again, the woman was still staring at him. In fact, she was looking him up and down appraisingly. The two men beside her grinned. It was one of those 'your flies are undone' moments, and Ianto's instinct was to look down and check. And that's when he first saw his own feet again. Not to mention everything else.

He reached out to the stationery cupboard, grabbed a notepad, and covered up his crotch.

'Lovely to see you, Mr Jones,' smiled the woman. She gestured to the conference table. 'Would you be more comfortable if you were seated?'

Ianto shuffled over and slid into a chair. He kept the pad of paper in his lap beneath the table.

His options appeared to be limited. There was no way past those big red-headed guys. The conference phone was within reach now – was there any way of dialling the Torchwood team fast enough before he was stopped? And what was the number for an outside line, anyway?

'Hello, my name is Jennifer Portland. Oh, well, I suppose you already know that.' She sat next to him and offered a handshake. It seemed rude not to accept it. The skin of her hand felt pale and cool, but her grip was firm.

Jennifer pulled one of the conference phones across the desk towards them. 'Right then,' she said briskly. 'Let's call up your friends in the car park, shall we?'

The wall of monitors sprang into life opposite them. It was displaying an image like a jigsaw with sixteen large rectangular pieces. In the centre was the Torchwood SUV, monitored from a pole-mounted CCTV camera. Wall speakers pulsed with the telephone's dial tone and the musical notes of the number going through.

'Hello?' answered Gwen's voice.

'Please stand by for a three-way call,' said Jennifer.

She tapped further numbers into the phone, and within half a minute she had connected a video call to the Hub. Toshiko's somewhat surprised face appeared in the upper-right flat-screen. 'Picture-in-picture,' whispered Jennifer to Ianto, as though she was doing a demo in an electrical shop.

Jennifer raised her voice to speak to the rest of the Torchwood team. 'Thank you for joining this conference call,' she said. 'We urgently need to talk about MonstaQuest. And as you've shown up in person…' At this, she couldn't resist a sidelong glance at Ianto's carefully positioned notepad. '… I think it's now my turn to reveal all.'

NINETEEN

Gwen hadn't expected it to be this easy to get into Achenbrite. A big red-headed guy, barrel-chested, big as a set of drawers, escorted her and Owen from the SUV and into the building. He'd not been surprised when they drew their handguns, and even raised his hands voluntarily like he was under arrest. She and Owen let him lead the way.

Their journey through the Achenbrite building ended in a luxuriously appointed conference room. On the way, Gwen had seen the bloody evidence of several violent struggles, including a gory side room full of mutilated corpses. A surveillance room just beyond where she now stood contained another dead man and a heaped pile of alien corpses.

When she settled into a chair at the head of the wide conference table, Gwen saw there were fresh scratches across its polished surface.

'Been in a fight?' she asked Ianto.

Ianto said he'd scratched the table when he threw a PDA onto it.

Gwen indicated his left arm. There were scrapes on Ianto's

skin, and his shoulder was smeared with dried blood. He licked his thumb and wiped ineffectually at the brown-red marks. 'That's where the bushes outside scratched me. These people haven't laid a finger on me.'

Jennifer Portland smiled benevolently at this reassurance. But her emotion seemed brittle. Gwen wasn't sure she liked her. The woman was in her mid-fifties, calm and composed in her seat beside Ianto. 'They haven't put any clothes on you, either,' responded Gwen tartly.

'He's got that A5 pad,' observed Owen. 'Or was he just doing dictation?'

Gwen nodded to the two red-headed men on the other side of Jennifer. They'd been introduced as Jennifer's sons, Chris and Matthew. They studied the Torchwood people sullenly. 'Didn't one of you have a spare boiler suit?'

'We've had more pressing problems than clothing,' Jennifer snapped. 'You'll have seen the people who died here today. Seven members of staff, including…' She paused for a little breath, regaining her composure. 'Including Toby. One of my sons. He was at the zoo.'

'Yeah, we saw something of him,' Owen said.

One of her other sons reached across and squeezed his mother's hand. Her only acknowledgement was a slight inclination of her head.

This smallest of gestures made Gwen feel more sorry for the woman. 'What happened here today?'

'Gareth.' Jennifer's voice was barely more than a whisper. 'I thought he was returning the device he'd stolen.'

'The catalogue thing?' prompted Gwen. 'Is that what brings the creatures through the Rift?'

Jennifer nodded. 'Three of them. A Hoix and a pair of Chantri Golems. They overwhelmed my team before they could respond. Chris and Matt managed to transfer them into the surveillance suite, and I flooded it with kolokine-7.'

Gwen looked at the nearby Monitor Room, nervously wondering whether the air seal on the door was impervious to alien toxic gases. 'In there?'

Jennifer nodded. 'Transmitted them into that room through the PDA's video signal, and asphyxiated them.'

'All right…' Jack's booming voice interrupted them. The image on the wall of flat-screen displays wobbled and steadied itself, resolving into a giant close-up of Jack and Toshiko. They were looking into a camera on Toshiko's desk back at the Hub. 'We're all set here.'

'What kept you?' asked Gwen.

'Wait and see,' he responded. 'OK, Mrs Portland. Whadda ya got?'

Jennifer looked up at Jack's image as it loomed over the whole room. 'We need to combine our resources, Captain Harkness.'

Jack's shook his head, a huge gesture on the display. 'You don't get it, Mrs Portland. You think you're in charge here, but you're not. You're really not.' He leaned in, and seemed bigger than ever. 'We know you've gotten your hands on some kind of alien tech. We know you've used it today in the mall and the zoo and in the centre of town. We know you tested it beforehand – an earlier visit to the zoo, a dogs' home…'

'A farm,' prompted Toshiko.

'Yeah, that poor guy is never gonna work out where his alpacas went. What were you hoping? To sell the stuff? Exploit it? Salvage what was left of your late husband's failing electronics firm?'

Gwen studied Jennifer's reaction. She didn't seem angry.

A kind of weary resignation hung on her pale face.

'Torchwood has been picking up the pieces of your "tests" for months,' Jack went on. 'And today, Achenbrite carelessly lost control of that device at the zoo. Nearly killed one of my officers. Nice to see ya, Ianto,' he added.

Jennifer's composure seemed to slip. 'If your officer here hadn't tampered with it, that device wouldn't have killed my Toby.'

'Are you *blaming* us?' Jack's tone was steely.

'I'm saying that it's not as simple as you make out.'

'Alien tech never is. Leave it to the experts.'

'Experts, indeed!' Jennifer Portland sniffed loudly. 'You've seen our work. We were able to control your communications network. We recognised your infiltration of our systems. And we have the equipment and expertise to contain the creatures from the Vandrogonite Visualiser.'

'Oh, wait a minute…' That had surprised Toshiko. 'Why do you call it that? Vandrogonite was just our best guess about its origins.'

'I know,' said Jennifer smoothly. She tapped at the keyboard built into the conference desk. One of the sixteen flat-screens changed to show a computer display.

'Picture-in-picture,' Ianto told Gwen.

'That's a Torchwood file,' said Toshiko in an aggrieved tone. 'You hacked our system?'

Ianto chuckled, then turned it into a cough. 'Not funny,' he said. 'Very serious, of course.'

Toshiko's head shifted slightly out of frame. Gwen could hear the clattering noise as she tapped furiously at her own keyboard.

'OK, we're officially impressed.' Jack settled more comfortably into the centre of the picture. 'So, where's the fire? You don't need us, right?' His sarcastic tone suggested otherwise.

Jennifer seemed to be taking a deep breath before speaking. 'Yes, Captain Harkness. We need your assistance.'

'And we should help you... why?'

'Because we have all of this.' Jennifer touch-typed a swift series of keystrokes.

Toshiko gave a cry of amazement. 'Wow!'

The computer display flat-screen now showed the three-dimensional rendering of the Achenbrite warehouse. Gwen recognised it from their planning session in the Hub. The difference was that the whole of the blue wireframe was alive with brighter spots of light, like a firestorm over the whole complex. And she knew that indicated Rift activity.

'I've turned off the non-disclosure field,' Jennifer explained.

Toshiko's head kept popping back into frame as she reeled off a list of what she could see. 'The whole place is awash with Rift energy. You've got dozens of pieces of alien tech... peak traces for recent incursions... residual hot spots where living creatures have penetrated...' Her voice trailed off incredulously.

'You're offering us this?' asked Jack. 'Because you sure ain't gonna fight us with it any more.'

'We weren't fighting you in the first place,' retorted Jennifer. 'We were trying to contain the damage done by Gareth.'

'We'll just take it all,' Jack replied coldly. 'Close you down. This isn't a negotiation. That's the lesson you've learned today, Mrs Portland.'

Jennifer slammed her palms down, and Gwen felt the angry vibrations through the conference table's surface. 'I don't need a lecture, I need your help. I want Gareth back.

I want my son. I've lost too many good men today from Achenbrite to care about anything other than that. We can't contain this any longer. Torchwood certainly can't, that much is clear from your fumbling attempts throughout the day. We need to work together.'

Jack leaned back in his chair and folded his arms. His image still dominated the room. Gwen saw something in that look. Maybe he wasn't telling them everything, but Jack could sometimes let his hurt pride get in the way of doing what was right.

So she leaned forward on the conference table and said to Jennifer: 'Tell me about Gareth.'

Jennifer's eyes darted to Gwen.

'Gareth?' Jack was saying on the screen. 'That's your son with the mental problems who's walking around town with a Vandrogonite Visualiser?'

'Jack!' snapped Gwen angrily. 'Just *listen* to her!' Sometimes, she thought, he really didn't get the whole Good Cop part of things. She smiled at Jennifer. 'Go on.'

Jennifer looked to her two sons. The woman who had seemed so in control when Gwen had first entered this conference room was now close to tears.

The older of the two sons, Chris, held her hand again. 'That Visualiser thing,' he said. 'It was part of our first find. Up at the Rhiwbina dig. We thought it was just an alien toy, y'know. And Gareth wasn't interested in Achenbrite.'

'Gareth's a sensitive lad,' interrupted his mother.

'Mum, he's not *right*,' Chris told her.

'Stop it!'

'Face it, Mum! Look at what he's done here. The mood swings, the obsessions… is it any wonder? None of us have ever been able to control him. You can't. Dad never could.'

'Don't speak that way of your dad. If he were alive today…'

'… he *still* wouldn't be able to control Gareth!' shouted Chris. 'He's unstable.' Now Chris was talking directly to Gwen. 'He loves his warcraft and his games and his computers, but he's got a gap up here when it comes to real people.' He tapped his own temple. 'You saw what he did to his girlfriend, didn't you?'

Gwen kept her expression neutral, though her heart was racing now. 'So what's been going on, Chris?'

'Gareth stole the Visualiser. Thought it was a toy. To be honest, it seemed harmless enough, and it kept him happy and out of our hair. He based that card game of his on the contents of the catalogue, set himself up in the garage where he was lodging. Got a lot of interest for MonstaQuest from toyshops and the Press. But then we saw the monsters started appearing for real…'

'And you thought you could just tidy up after him,' said Jack. Gwen could feel the cold anger in his words. 'Achenbrite are way out of their depth here. That Vandrogonite device is fuelled by *emotions*. The MonstaQuest cards just add to the excitement. And Gareth's unstable. You gave a blow torch to a pyromaniac.'

'No, worse than that,' said Ianto. He emphasised his point with urgent hand gestures above the conference table. The writing pad slipped from his lap, but he no longer cared. 'Gareth isn't controlling that thing any more. He thinks he is, but it's *using* him. Those flowers you found at the mall, Tosh? They were here too, in the corridor. Alien flora. It's like the device is trying to create the ideal environment for the creatures it brings through.'

'Oh boy,' murmured Jack. 'Terraforming. Or whatever the

Vandrogonite word for it is. Creating an alien world right here in Cardiff.'

'There's something else,' said the other son, Matt. Gwen couldn't decide whether he sounded more worried or ashamed than his brother. The big man was shuffling in his seat, almost absurdly. He reminded her of a naughty toddler caught out in a lie. 'The transmission frequency.'

Gwen looked blank. 'The what?'

'That Visualiser thing,' said Matt, 'has an affinity for other devices that transmit visuals. You know, CCTV, video phones that kind of thing. If the conditions are just right, the creatures can be transmitted to another receiving device.'

'That makes sense,' piped up Toshiko from the video wall.

Everyone in the room stared at her image. Toshiko blinked back at them worriedly.

'Oh, for goodness sake!' cried Gwen, exasperated. 'There are no Rift creatures in here at the moment.' She chewed her lip worriedly. 'Are there?'

'You're missing the point,' Jack told her. 'You said it yourself, Gwen: Torchwood can control small groups of scavengers for day trips to Cardiff. Even Achenbrite can stop some of those.' If he could see the dirty looks that the Portland family were giving him, he just ignored it. 'But use this Visualiser near any passing camera phone, and Gareth's got something that'll give numberless creatures a season ticket to anywhere on Earth. We gotta find him!' He must have noticed that Toshiko was doing her 'aha' face again, because he turned to her and asked: 'Got something?'

Toshiko rattled some more commands on her keyboard. Part of the wall display changed into the interface of an audio player. The sound of a radio interview began to play through the conference room speakers. Gwen saw from Toshiko's smile that she was enjoying making a point: she had not only regained control of the Torchwood computer, but she was now able to manipulate the Achenbrite systems remotely.

David Brigstocke's voice filled the room. Jack rolled his eyes, but Toshiko made a shushing gesture and indicated that they should listen.

Brigstocke was concluding a live radio link from the centre of Cardiff. He was interviewing celebrity shopper Martina Baldachi. From the edge to his voice it was clear he thought the assignment below his dignity. The Italian supermodel was in town because her husband, Jakob, was playing in the international between AC Liguria and Cardiff United. She'd taken their son, Galileo, to Wendleby's toy store. Brigstocke prompted her to say some platitudes about the terrible traffic accident just outside the store, and Martina turned the interview into a bit of a car crash by explaining that they'd missed the whole thing because their chauffeur-driven limousine had taken them to privileged access at the rear of the store.

Was there a note of smug satisfaction in Brigstocke's voice? 'Looks like Galileo has a memento of his trip today. You bought him a pack of cards instead of a toy telescope.'

'Oh no,' purred Martina. 'He has heard all about these MonstaQuest cards. He is so pleased to meet the man who invented them. Thank you so much, Gareth.'

'You're welcome,' said a young man's voice.

'Gareth!' breathed his mother as she listened to him over the conference room speakers.

Brigstocke was explaining to radio listeners now that Gareth was wearing his Cardiff United shirt, but had just accepted a couple of VIP tickets for the match from the captain of the rival team. Jack was evidently too busy to enjoy the humour of this, because he was watching Toshiko's agitated reaction to some other data that she'd received.

'Electromagnetic spectrum analysis,' Toshiko explained. She muted the audio, and displayed a schematic of Cardiff.

Slap bang in the city centre was Wendleby's department store. And all around that, the Rift energy was going off the scale.

TWENTY

Ianto Jones hated waiting. He stared out between the front seats of the Achenbrite van and tried to stay calm.

Chris Portland fidgeted in the driver's seat, his mother next to him. Beside Ianto in the rear, Matt Portland stared fixedly at a scanner. The back of the vehicle had barely enough room for one person, crammed as it was with badly wired equipment and alien tech. If he didn't die from an electrical shock, Ianto reckoned he might keel over from asphyxiation.

'Chris, have you farted?' grumbled Matt.

Matt snorted. 'Why you asking me instead of that Torchwood tosser?'

'Don't be rude about our guest,' said Jennifer. She had been agitated throughout the journey, and now drummed her manicured nails in a staccato rhythm on the dash in front of her.

They were parked at the ideal spot – close to a local electricity substation, and within sight of the nearest mobile phone relay. They were ready to kill the cellular network by disabling the base transceiver station. And, if necessary, they could cut off power to the Wendleby's store through remote access to its systems and the local grid.

The Achenbrite team made it clear they thought they were in charge. Ianto was happy to let them think that.

The cadence of Jennifer's tapping faltered. 'Oh, I can't wait around here any longer,' she sighed. 'Not while Gareth is in trouble.' Before anyone could stop her, she had slipped out through the passenger door and slammed it shut behind her.

Ianto reached up to tap his earcomm into action. In a blur of speed, Matt Portland's hand seized Ianto's arm. 'Radio silence.'

'Why, who do you think is listening in?' Ianto used his free hand to pinch the nerve points on the other man's wrist and pulled it away.

He peered through the front windscreen, and could just make out Jennifer's red hair as the woman disappeared into the shopping crowds.

Ianto activated his earcomms. 'Mrs Portland is moving. She's on her way into Wendleby's.'

Martina Baldachi hated the general public. She was desperate to get out of Wendleby's.

The photo op had finished. Martina and her entourage were making their way down the emergency stairs at the rear of the store. The limo would be waiting for them, engine running, in the loading area at the rear of the store. Her bodyguard, Carlo, led the way, which frustrated the store manager who was trying to chaperone his VIP guests. The manager was a fussy man in a cheap suit, and Martina wouldn't be sorry if she never saw him again. She'd already forgotten his name.

Martina was furious with her personal assistant, Andrea. Where was the TV coverage? Why was there only a handful of Press photographers? Didn't they know who she was? Hadn't she brought Galileo with her? The store manager was apologising about some bus that had crashed at the front of the store, because it had drawn most of the Press away. Andrea was concentrating on helping Galileo negotiate the stairs, and said nothing.

Carlo had stopped on the stair landing, confronted by two strangers. Martina's first instinct, as usual, was that she was about to be kidnapped. Sensing her fear, Galileo shrank back too. He anxiously sought out Andrea's hand, not his mother's.

The first stranger was a pale-faced man with bad hair and a cruel mouth. The other one was a dark-haired woman, who obviously had more style. They identified themselves.

'Bloody Torchwood,' said the store manager.

The dark-haired Torchwood woman saw Martina on the higher stair and smiled in recognition. 'Hello, it's Martina Baldachi, isn't it? My fiancé is a big fan of your husband's. My name's Gwen Cooper and this—'

'One autograph,' snapped Martina. 'We must leave for our car.' What a pity, she thought. This Torchwood woman really should get something done about her fringe.

'Sorry,' said Gwen Cooper. 'You misunderstand. We're looking for the man you gave those VIP tickets to earlier.'

Martina clicked her fingers in Andrea's face. 'Tickets.'

'Owen Harper,' said the pale-faced man. He moved up a few steps to talk to her. 'We don't want your tickets. We want to find Gareth Portland. Where is he?'

Gareth? She remembered an untidy young man in the toy department. She'd given him VIP tickets to the match. Not for the private box that she'd be in, obviously. The smelly Welsh oaf would be in a separate section with all the other freeloaders, leaving her to make her phone calls in peace and not require her to look interested during the match. Perhaps something could be rescued from this PR disaster, she began to think, so long as the cameras saw her entering the Stadium.

Owen Harper was still talking, 'Listen, love, I can see you're in a rush to get to your next colonic or whatever. So let us know where you saw Gareth, and we'll get out of your fabulously coiffured hair.'

Martina drew back her manicured hand and slapped him across the face.

The thin man's hand moved like lightning. It seized Martina's wrist so that her hand remained pressed against his cheek. It was both intimate and threatening.

Carlo twisted around to defend her, reaching for the gun that he should not have been carrying. But the Torchwood woman turned the movement into a shove that pressed the bodyguard against the grey brick of the service corridor. Carlo grunted in pain as the woman pushed his arm further up his back.

Martina blinked in fear. The thin man's eyes glittered at her, demanding an answer. 'Gareth? He was in the toy department,' she blustered.

'On the fourth floor,' added the store manager.

'Thank you,' said Owen Harper. He let go of Martina's hand, and pushed on past her up the stairs. Gwen Cooper released Carlo, and followed Harper. As the pair disappeared around the next corner, Martina could hear the man mocking his colleague. 'Ooh, my fiancé is *such* a big fan…'

Martina snatched Galileo's hand from Andrea's grasp,

and practically fled down the remaining stairs. She pulled up her fur collar and ran to the white stretch limo that waited patiently in the loading bay. The afternoon air was warmer than she'd expected. After all, that thin man had only just come into the building, and his face and fingers had been icy cold.

Toshiko hated driving in town. She gripped the wheel of her 350Z, and focused on the road while Jack grumbled next to her.

Usually, she let the others take charge of whatever vehicle they were using, while she remained in the Hub to coordinate activities, or used the remote systems in the rear of the SUV. She didn't like the idea of Jack driving her car today

'Can't this thing go any faster?' Jack was an irritable passenger at the best of times. Today, he was itching to get on and get out. 'Did you choose this car? I bet I could get it into fourth gear.'

'Your gear-change foot might make that difficult.'

Jack flexed his left leg. 'Well, I bet I could get it above thirty.'

Toshiko tried to focus on the late-afternoon traffic. 'You're not on my insurance,' she said feebly.

'You mean you don't trust me with your car.' Jack sounded faintly offended.

Toshiko considered some polite lies. 'I mean I don't trust you with my car,' she admitted eventually.

The front of Wendleby's was still blocked to through traffic. Toshiko flicked on the blue warning lights in her windshield, and the police team lifted the barrier so that she could drive through.

'Hey, there's a big picture of a Weevil in that window,' Jack noted. 'When did that become NFC?'

Toshiko looked blankly at him.

'Normal For Cardiff,' explained Jack. 'Remember when we had to cover up every Weevil appearance? Looks like MonstaQuest has made them mainstream.'

'I'd be more worried about that Halloween display in the next window,' Toshiko told him. She even shivered a little.

Jack checked it out. 'What… you're frightened of clowns?'

'They're scary clowns,' she muttered defensively. 'Like Stephen King's "It" clown.'

'Yeah, but…' Jack was grinning. 'Clowns?'

Toshiko pretended to ignore him as she steered around the building and into the loading bay. A white stretch limo squeezed past them on its way out. Toshiko parked the 350Z next to the Torchwood SUV.

'I'm going in,' said Jack. 'Looks like Gwen and Owen are already here. You can base yourself in the SUV.'

With that, he struggled from the car and limped into the building.

Jennifer Portland hated people being rude. She called over to the policeman who was at the crash barrier, but he seemed to be ignoring her.

'Excuse me,' she called to him, 'I need to get into the store.'

The constable had taken off his cap and was scratching idly at his blond hair. He was engrossed in his conversation with another officer. 'It was going to be bad enough on crowd patrol for the match,' he told her, 'but this is just madness.'

'Yeah, right, Andy,' she laughed. 'You're just sore because you haven't got touchline duty for the international.' The female officer had spotted Jennifer now. 'Sorry, madam. You can't come through here. There's been an accident. As you can probably see.'

'The overturned bus would have been your first clue,' the policeman muttered under his breath.

Jennifer could certainly see. Even without the crash barriers, the street was mostly blocked by the mangled wreckage of a bendy bus. Soil and debris showed where it must have struck some road works and tipped over before smashing into the front window of Wendleby's. An accident investigation team had set up floodlights in anticipation of dusk. The blue flashing lights of the remaining ambulance speckled the area. A large crane was slowly manoeuvring itself into position on the far side.

Jennifer smiled politely at the officer, and turned away. No point in arguing, and no time for it either. She took a slim cylinder from her handbag, no bigger than a lipstick. Its surface looked like wet tar, but the device felt firm and dry between her fingers. Jennifer didn't know which alien race had created it. She only knew what it could do.

She squeezed the device, and it buzzed quietly. When Jennifer turned to the police officers again, she saw them twist away, nauseated. When they faced towards her, the feeling got worse. Once they turned away, the effect reduced.

Jennifer slipped under the barrier and marched towards the store. She avoided looking at the blood and glass that spilled from the broken-backed bus, keeping her eyes on the shop displays instead. One large window was filled with Halloween costumes – cackling witches, illuminated pumpkins, and some cruel-faced clowns with fangs in their huge red mouths. The next window was decorated with cartoon monsters, and a poster that declared: 'MonstaQuest

Demonstration Today. Wendleby's Toy Department, Fourth Floor.'

She pushed through the barrier that had been placed inside the store to prevent customers leaving by the exits nearest to the accident. The late-afternoon shopping crowds had not diminished, and Jennifer used the nausea device to part the crowds and make her way to the escalators unimpeded.

As she negotiated the top of the second-floor escalator, an old man in a pork pie hat became wildly disoriented by the nausea device, and staggered into her. The device jolted out of her hand, bounced once on the rubber handrail, and dropped into the down escalator. Jennifer dithered for a moment at the top of the up escalator, undecided about whether to try and retrieve the device.

The crowd behind her began to recover their composure, a continuous stream of people pushing past as they continued onto the floor. No time, decided Jennifer. She had to press on, and reach the fourth floor. Reach Gareth before Torchwood did.

David Brigstocke hated the crush of Saturday shopping. But today, he decided, he hated Eleri Francis even more.

This was a trivial news assignment, and he believed Eleri must have known that. He was supposed to be covering the aftermath of the bus crash in the street outside, but his editor had sent him into the store and up to the toy department instead. One of the Wendleby's staff had phoned the radio news office with a tip-off that Martina Baldachi had been spotted buying gifts. More likely one of Martina's PRs had tipped them off. 'Send Ieuan Walters,' countered Brigstocke. 'Isn't that why we have an Entertainment Correspondent?' This was the same old office bullshit. It had been like this since he'd overheard them talking about him in the canteen, in Welsh, stupidly assuming that he couldn't understand. They'd understood him, all right, after Brigstocke confronted them and explained what he thought of them. In Welsh.

'Ieuan's at the Mid-Wales Beer Festival in Llanwrtyd Wells,' Eleri had replied. 'You'll find the toy department on the fourth floor.'

Brigstocke had managed to have a bit of fun at Martina Baldachi's expense during the interview. That wouldn't go down well with Eleri, he supposed, but with a live feed it was too late for her to do anything about that. Now he was on a down escalator, evaluating whether he still had time to get to the crash site, when he spotted a familiar figure hobbling into the store.

Captain Jack Harkness.

Brigstocke caught up with him by the service lift.

'It won't come any faster if you keep pressing the button like that.'

Brigstocke was pleased to see Harkness's exasperated reaction.

'Kinda busy.'

'As always,' replied Brigstocke. 'You're looking good for someone whose foot was almost severed at the zoo.' He watched Harkness involuntarily look at his own left foot. 'I spoke to the paramedics, Jack. You can't fool medical professionals about that kind of thing.'

Harkness gave up on the service lift, and limped across to the escalator instead. He paused before stepping on. At first, Brigstocke thought he was being cautious about his injured foot. Until he realised that Harkness wasn't entirely sure where he was going.

'You want to help?' Harkness had narrowed his eyes,

looking for a reaction. He leaned in close to speak into Brigstocke's ear. 'That kid you were interviewing earlier? He's a terrorist suspect, and we need to track him down. No, put the digital recorder down.'

'It's a phone,' said Brigstocke. 'I'm calling the police.'

Harkness closed his hands over the phone, folding the casing shut in Brigstocke's palm. 'We *are* the police.'

'No you're not. I've talked to the police about Torchwood.'

'Do you want to help or not?'

Brigstocke licked his lips as he pondered this. Across the aisle from them a customer lift dinged as it arrived at their floor. Brigstocke put his phone back in his jacket pocket. 'Toy department. Fourth floor.'

Brigstocke jumped into the lift and held the door, gesturing for Harkness to join him. As well as helping, it kept him close to his quarry.

Harkness limped over. Before he got in, he tapped at his ear and said: 'Ianto? Hold off for a couple of minutes.'

Gareth Portland hated everyone. They bustled past him where he sat at his stand on the fourth floor, unconcerned whether he was alive or dead.

But he was so alive. More than he had ever been in his whole life.

The Visualiser purred in his hand. It spoke to him. Reassured him. Knew him. Loved him.

The world moved past Gareth Portland, uncaring. So it was time for the world to change.

TWENTY-ONE

When Jennifer Portland saw her son sitting alone in the toy department, she thought her heart would finally break.

All around this area of the sales floor, eager children squealed with delight as their parents guided them through the toy displays. But there was no clamour about the MonstaQuest sales stand. Gareth sat to one side of it in a bucket seat. Stacked piles of unsold card packs teetered beside him. His head was bowed, and he was studying his hands. It brought back sharp and painful memories of seeing her teenage son at home, after another awful day at his savage Secondary, slumped in an uncommunicative heap at the dinner table.

The MonstaQuest stand was flanked by two cardboard monsters. They were exaggerated caricatures from the pack, blown up to life size, standing guard, designed to attract customers. Jennifer recognised them as a Weevil and a Hoix.

She approached quietly. Gareth was studying the VIP tickets he'd been given for the international match. A couple of students strolled up to pester him.

'I'm on a break,' Gareth told them without looking up. Jennifer suddenly realised how long it was since she'd heard his voice.

The students wanted to buy the tickets from him. Gareth responded not by looking at the students but by clutching the tickets to his chest. It was a protective gesture that Jennifer recognised from his childhood, that she'd seen him do with a favourite toy.

'They're not for sale,' Gareth said.

'Come on, Harry,' one of the students said to his mate, tugging his arm. 'We'll have to try the touts instead.' He kicked the leg of Gareth's chair. 'Don't want your lousy tickets, mate.'

'Or your stupid card game,' added Harry. He prodded one of the stacked piles of MonstaQuest cards, and it toppled over against the foot of the Hoix.

Gareth stood up angrily, but the students had already strolled off. Jennifer saw a murderous look in her son's eyes. She'd seen that in the Achenbrite CCTV cameras earlier. It was a cold, unspoken fury that warned of coming violence the way that dark clouds threatened rain.

The Visualiser device was in Gareth's hands. It was only when he looked up again that he saw his mother watching.

Jennifer walked over to him. 'Come on, Gareth,' she said soothingly. 'Time to stop all this.'

Gareth stared at her like she was a stranger.

Gwen was still giggling at Owen in the cargo lift.

Owen didn't find it funny. 'Well, it looked real enough to me.'

'Don't worry, Owen. It's definitely dead now.'

A cardboard Weevil lay crumpled in the corner, the

remains of a MonstaQuest display item. Owen had taken one look at it as they were about to board the lift and put a bullet through its forehead. Gwen's first reaction was to duck from the ricochet. Her second was to burst out laughing.

'It was coming towards me,' persisted Owen.

'It was falling over,' Gwen corrected him. 'It's funny, but when you're embarrassed you don't blush any more.' She looked more closely at his cheek where Martina Baldachi had whacked him. 'Did that hurt?'

'Didn't feel a thing,' Owen said. 'Hope it doesn't bruise, though. Don't want to spend the rest of my death with fingerprints across my face.'

The lift bell pinged.

'Fourth floor,' said Owen. 'Kitchenware, furniture, children's toys, and alien technology.'

Before the doors slid open, there was a mighty thump against the other side, accompanied by angry shouting.

'Keep your hair on!' called Owen. 'They won't open any faster if…'

His voice trailed off as the doors parted. Beyond the lift, two huge gorillas were hurling furniture across the sales floor. Gorillas in alien uniforms. Terrified shoppers and Wendleby's staff were scrambling to get through or over the displays and away to safety.

Gwen unholstered her handgun. Owen was ahead of her, already out of the lift and stepping over the remains of the coffee table that had been hurled against the outer doors.

One of the creatures broke off from its bombardment, and swung onto a tall, freestanding unit. Racks of cutlery tumbled off and clattered to the floor. A young sales assistant stood below it, petrified. One of her friends seized a skillet from a display of pans and lashed out wildly. The gorilla casually reached out one long arm and simply batted him away into a rack of electrical goods.

Owen waved away some shoppers who had raced from the next department to see what all the noise was. One woman was struggling with her many bags of shopping, while her husband yanked the sleeve of her coat and told her to leave them. The short argument was abruptly ended when the nearest gorilla landed right in front of them with a thump, opened its huge mouth and bellowed a savage roar straight into their faces. The woman shrieked, flung her shopping aside, and fled. The gorilla began to pick curiously at the abandoned Wendleby's bags.

Two other shoppers were angling their mobile phone cameras at the creature. 'Are you insane?' Owen yelled. Before he could reach them, there was a swirl of brilliant white light from over by the sofa beds, and one of the gorillas melted away into nothing.

Owen rushed up to the nearest shopper, a bristle-headed lad in a bomber jacket who bore an uncanny resemblance to the gorillas. He smacked the camera phone from the lad's hand. 'That could have been the last picture you ever took.'

'It will be if you smashed my camera, you jerk!' He was bunching his fists, squaring up to Owen.

Owen held up his compact double-action 9mm pistol so that the lad could see it clearly. 'Talk to the gun, 'cause the face ain't listening.' He was pleased to see the bloke was shocked into silence. 'Get out of here before you're killed. Could be that thing that does it, could be me.' Owen switched on his earcomms. 'Ianto, you there, mate?'

'Receiving.'

'Take out the mobile phone network.'

'Doing it now.' Ianto's voice crackled in his ear. 'Got some

212

activity up there?'

Gwen was in on the conversation now. 'We might need back-up. Are those Achenbrite boys on standby with their capture equipment? These things look like the biggest gorillas you ever saw.'

'Gorillas?' said Ianto. 'You don't see many of those in Wendleby's.'

'They're not picking out fabrics,' said Gwen. 'They're in combat gear.'

'Oh,' said Ianto. 'So they'd be guerrilla gorillas, then?'

'Just send Achenbrite up here, Ianto.'

The remaining gorilla bellowed from its position atop the display unit. It swung its hairy, drooling face around, and its scrunched expression suggested that it couldn't work out where its monstrous mate had gone.

'I used to love a bit of a shop, me,' sighed Gwen as she took aim. Her bullet struck the monster right between the eyes. It fell backwards off the display and clattered down into a display of coffee makers and kettles.

Owen hurried over to where it had fallen. A small crowd of frightened people edged nearer to it. The gorilla heaved one last great gust of rank air, and its final breath sprayed the crowd with snot from its huge nostrils. The crowd cowered. A handful stared at their mobile phones as though they could will them into action, but the handsets had died as abruptly as the creature. Owen could hear the three-note apology from the nearest ones, and the calm Achenbrite statement.

'What's going on?' demanded the lad in the bomber jacket. Owen held up his gun as a fresh warning, and the bloke looked shocked again. Except this time, it was at something behind Owen.

He whirled to face a new threat. A spindly creature with

a tiny central body and etiolated limbs staggered across the furniture department. It trailed its dangling hands almost lazily over a nearby sofa bed. The cover split open and spewed stuffing and springs, as if it had been eviscerated. The creature flicked its head from side to side quizzically, reached out one long arm, and plucked at a ceiling-mounted CCTV camera.

'Shit!' spat Owen. 'Ianto, you have to kill the CCTV!'

He loosed off a couple of shots. The creature picked up a two-seater sofa and flipped it across the room. It could have been made of feathers for all the effort it seemed to require. But it felt heavy enough when it glanced off Owen and knocked the gun from his hand. Gwen took a harder blow, and fell beneath the sofa.

The creature stalked closer. A sales assistant got in the way, so it picked him up and flexed its fingers. The man's body was severed, and the two halves of his corpse were discarded like litter. Blood sprayed over the nearby furnishings.

The creature moved towards Owen. He scrabbled backwards, desperate to get away from the knife-edged talons.

It brought its insectoid head closer to him, so close that he could see his face reflected in its compound eyes. Was it looking at him? Scenting him? About to devour him?

He didn't have time to speculate any more, because the head split open in an explosion of dark liquid.

When Owen opened his eyes, Jack Harkness was grinning down at him. One hand held his .38 Webley revolver, which was still smoking. The other was held out to help Owen get to his feet.

'I can't believe all of this, Jack.' The stranger beside Jack sported a tweed jacket and a Welsh accent.

'Who's your mate?' Owen asked Jack.

Jack clapped the stranger on the shoulder. 'David Brigstocke, from BBC Radio Wales. Gimme a hand, David, I think one of my officers is trapped over here. She looks good in leather, but not when it's on a sofa.'

Owen assisted them in freeing Gwen from beneath the tumbled heap of furniture. 'He's your journalist?'

'He wanted to do a "day in the life" piece, I said he could tag along.' Jack was staring at the ceiling-mounted cameras. 'Why are these cameras still operational?'

Ianto's voice said in their ears: 'I'm having a bit of trouble isolating the feeds.'

'Take out the power to the whole place!' shouted Jack.

The journalist, Brigstocke, looked alarmed. 'Shouldn't we evacuate the store first?'

'We?' smiled Jack. He indicated the shrinking crowds around them. 'Besides, I think they've got the message. OK, David. Until the power goes out, let's make sure they're keeping clear of this area. Go and hit the reverses on the up escalators. Then call all the lifts to this floor and jam their doors open. Prevents anyone getting trapped inside them.'

Owen saw that Brigstocke was hesitating by the torn remains of the store clerk.

'Hey!' Jack snapped at Brigstocke. 'You wanted to be a part of this… Go!'

The toy department was deserted now. Most of the shoppers had been parents, accompanying their bright-eyed children to plan Christmas. Thinking about birthday presents. The occasional weekend dad making up for his workday absence with the bribe of a gift. Mothers and fathers whose parental instinct was to protect their children first of all.

So when a whirlwind of savage animals had sprung from the MonstaQuest display, it had rapidly become obvious that this wasn't a store event. That much was clear from the genuine terror in the staff, who had abandoned their desks and tills and fled the scene screaming like everyone else. Two huge gorillas had lumbered off, dragging their feet and knuckles, whooping and chattering at the new sights. A whirlwind group of huge, savage insects hovered and chittered in the deserted toy department, plucking at the soft toys as though considering how edible they were.

Parents, children, staff had fled. Now there was only one mother left. And it was her instinct to stay with her child.

Jennifer Portland faced Gareth at the heart of the storm, trying to ignore the wafts from the dreadful creatures that fluttered over her head, the slashing sounds of their razor-sharp mandibles.

'What have you done, Gareth?' She pleaded with him to look at her, to acknowledge her. But he simply stared out with a cold and dispassionate look at the devastation he had wrought.

As her son had grown up, Jennifer had been able to tell when Gareth was distressed. Even when he wouldn't tell her, she could recognise the set of his mouth, or the particular way he slouched when he tried to explain something, or the sparkle of unshed tears in his frustrated eyes. Now as she looked at him, she didn't recognise anything at all. It was like the shell of her beloved son. All that was of him had been emptied out and replaced with something else.

'What have you done?' she asked again.

That was when all the store lights went out.

The noise from the monstrous insects all around them dipped momentarily, before resuming with a new, angry intensity.

There was still a sharp source of light across the sales floor. It spilled out from within the MonstaQuest display behind Gareth, throwing his outline into sharp silhouette. He was staring at the Visualiser device. He turned it to the light so he could read the display, but what Jennifer could read was the fury in her son's face.

'Not enough people!' snarled Gareth. 'Insufficient power!'

'Gareth, come back to me!' pleaded Jennifer. She shuffled closer. Desperate to hold him. To forgive him.

'There is no Gareth,' said the thing that had been her son. Its black eyes bored into her. 'And besides, you were already dead to him.'

Gareth strode past his mother, shrugging off her attempt to grab him, to hug him. She turned to follow him as he left. But the insect creatures had gathered in front of her. Gareth was already out of the room when the insects fell upon Jennifer.

Gwen intercepted Ianto and the Portland brothers as they struggled up the final set of fire stairs. The Achenbrite pair were laden with capture equipment, and unable to use the escalators because Brigstocke had reversed the direction so that they only travelled down and out of the store.

The store's back-up generator had kicked in, offering low-level emergency lighting. When they reached the toy department, they found that Jack and Owen had already picked their way across the debris. David Brigstocke hovered behind them nervously.

There was no sign of Gareth Portland. A fading glow around the MonstaQuest stand illuminated a group of four huge insect creatures that huddled over something.

With a thrill of horror, Gwen recognised that the something was Jennifer Portland.

Matt Portland had noticed this too. He let out a howl of anguish and rage, and started to charge at the creatures. Between them, Owen and Gwen managed to hold him back.

'I'm sorry,' Gwen told him. 'So sorry, but it's too late for her. You have to help your brother set up the capture equipment.'

The insects were losing interest in Jennifer's body, but the noise from these newcomers had attracted their attention. One of them opened its wings and flitted up to the ceiling. The other three twisted to look at their new prey, and their mandibles champed in anticipation.

'Stand back!' shouted Chris. He and his brother had angled the capture equipment at the larger group of insects, and the devices hummed into life. A static crackle filled the air, and the bulbous ends of the Achenbrite rifles spat out a cloudy spray that enveloped their targets. The three insects twisted, shrieked, and dwindled in size.

'Get them in the box!' Chris called out to his brother.

But Matt threw the capture box aside, and ran over to the three shrunken insect creatures. His face was contorted with utter fury and he slammed down the end of his rifle against them. The insects splattered under the assault, a yellow-green stain smeared on the carpet tiles. Matt continued to pound at the gooey remains until he slumped down exhausted, his rifle a useless, mangled mess beside him.

The remaining insect shrieked its anger, and swooped down at Chris Portland. The Achenbrite man stumbled back, tumbling over a display case of Disney characters. The monstrous insect snatched at the plush characters, slicing them with the ends of its sharp legs. Shreds of material and stuffing scattered over the floor. Chris stumbled free, and brought up his rifle to fire.

The end of it was crushed and bent out of shape. He fired anyway, but the rifle smoked and sparked in his hands, and he had to throw it aside.

A fusillade of shots rang out. The Torchwood team had all taken aim at the insect. Their bullets pinged off its carapace, barely scratching the creature but ricocheting in all directions.

The creature rose into the air and menaced them from above.

Jack was already activating his earcomm. 'Tosh? Plan B. Did Ianto patch things through to you?'

'Yes.'

'OK, bring the cellular network back online.' Jack waggled his hand urgently at David Brigstocke. 'Gimme your camera phone.'

Brigstocke fumbled in his tweed jacket and finally produced the item.

Jack's fingers fiddled with the phone interface. He angled its camera lens up at the looming insect. 'Get back, all of you.'

When they all moved, the insect motioned to follow them.

'No you don't!' snapped Jack, and began to hurl Disney characters at the creature. It swooped down at him, slashing at his arm with a razor-edged leg.

'That's more like it!' he grinned, nursing the wound with one hand while keeping the camera aimed at the insect. 'C'mon, c'mon! You've got nowhere to escape to.'

The creature reared back, ready to strike. Before vanishing

in a swirling cloud of brilliant illumination.

Gwen stepped forward hesitantly. 'Where did it go, Jack?'

Jack snapped the phone shut, and tossed it back to Brigstocke. 'Before we left, Tosh set up a video phone in the Hub dungeon. That insect will materialise in secure storage down there, and we can deal with it later.' His smile faded. 'Assuming I dialled it right.' He rapidly muttered a mobile phone number as though checking his memory.

Gwen blanched. 'That's Rhys's number!'

Jack was grinning again. 'Just kidding.'

She slapped his arm. 'I hope he's safely on his way to the international, by now.'

No such joy for the Portlands, she reflected. Just across from her, Matt was weeping over his mother's remains. Chris stoically tried to ignore this, as though that would deny the truth of it. He carefully sprayed the area around the MonstaQuest stand with weed killer. Gwen went to him and saw the shrivelled stalks of the same alien plants that they'd seen in the shopping mall. The bizarre foliage surrounded a huge gash in the surface, so wide and deep that she could see right through to the third floor below.

'Gareth was using the Visualiser to recreate an alien world for those creatures,' said Jack from beside her.

'Why did he stop?'

'Not enough power.'

Gwen studied Jack's face in the flicker of the store's emergency lighting. 'Because we cut the electricity?'

'No. Because the store evacuated,' said Jack. 'Not enough terrified witnesses to give it the emotional oomph it needs.'

'Better track him down, then. He's still got that Visualiser thing. And he can find more people just by leaving the store.'

'Couple of other things too,' said Jack. 'Tosh, how many of the creatures got away through mobile phone calls?'

'There were seventy-nine calls from those coordinates,' Toshiko's voice replied. 'Only... let's see... one of them was synchronised with a spike in Rift energy, and I got GPS coordinates for the destination phone.'

Gwen nodded. 'The gorilla thing we saw.'

'OK, Tosh,' said Jack briskly. 'Send the coordinates through to Owen. Gwen, you guys know what you're looking for. Capture or kill. You can phone it through to the Hub, if you need to.' He turned to the others. 'Ianto, you and the Portlands need to do some clean-up here.'

'Clean-up?' snapped Brigstocke. His composure seemed to be returning. 'So this is how it works, is it Jack?'

Jack ignored him, and spoke instead to Ianto. 'Make sure the Portlands are OK,' he murmured.

Gwen saw that Jack passed a blister pack of Retcon pills to Ianto before he left the toy department.

Toshiko was ready and waiting for Jack in the SUV. The window wound down, and she leaned out to talk to him as he approached.

'Any easy way of tracking Gareth through town?' Jack asked.

She looked apologetic. 'We took out the power for the whole block. CCTV is completely down.'

'Rift traces?'

She shook her head. 'Place is awash with what you were dealing with on the fourth floor.' She held up a metallic square. 'Could try this?'

Jack wasn't sure he liked the idea of Toshiko using the other Vandrogonite Visualiser. 'How difficult can it be to find a guy wandering round Cardiff in an orange T-shirt?' He clicked his tongue as he became aware that Brigstocke had caught up with him.

'You're really not much of a football fan, are you?' said the journalist. He beckoned for Jack to walk a short distance down the access road to the main shopping street.

There was a guy in an orange T-shirt.

Oh.

There were seven more. And another group of five. And two of those were women.

'Cardiff United shirts,' Brigstocke grinned.

Jack closed his eyes and took a deep, calming breath.

'But I know where he'll be,' said Brigstocke. When Jack opened his eyes again, the journalist was standing very close to him. 'Take me with you, and I'll show you.'

He refused to say more until he was sitting in the passenger seat of the SUV. Toshiko sat in the rear, fiddling with her Visualiser.

'OK, where?' asked Jack.

'You're *really* not a football fan, are you?' said Brigstocke. 'He's got tickets for the international. He looked *really* pleased to get them. So, he's headed for the Millennium Stadium. That's where Cardiff United play their home fixtures. I've covered loads of events,' he added quickly. 'I have Press accreditation, and I know my way around the place.'

Jack wasn't convinced. 'I think Gareth has other things on his mind right now. All he has to do is use that Visualiser in the middle of some crowd of terrified late-night shoppers.'

'How about a capacity crowd at the Millennium Stadium?' asked Brigstocke. 'That's over 70,000 highly emotional spectators. And did you say these things can be transmitted through visuals?'

Jack nodded.

'Better get a move on, then.' Brigstocke started to buckle his seat belt. 'They have a live international television feed.'

TWENTY-TWO

Getting out of the loading area and past the crashed bus proved to be the easiest part of their journey.

The closer they got to their destination, the slower their progress became. The Stadium loomed in the distance, the support towers around it looking like the crooked legs of an enormous grasshopper. Jack tried not to think what sort of monstrous insect life Gareth Portland might conjure up inside it.

Spectators flooded the streets on their way to the match. They were indifferent to the SUV's display of blue lights, and slapped the side of the vehicle as it attempted to pass through them.

In the passenger seat, Brigstocke flicked through a MonstaQuest pack that Jack had snatched from the stand at Wendleby's. He spread them out over his knees, and considered their contents. 'Some gruesome sorts here, Jack. Are they all real?'

Toshiko peered through from the rear of the SUV. 'Many of them are. But a handful of them were just made up by Gareth when he created the game. The weather cards, for instance.' She held up a MonstaQuest Whirlwind card. 'They're all based on Earth meteorology. And those guerrilla gorillas? They're more of a pun. Something Gareth added in as a joke.'

'The people they killed in Wendleby's weren't laughing,' Jack observed.

'No, that's my point, really,' Toshiko continued. 'I don't think that the Visualiser is bringing them through the Rift. I think it's creating them from scratch. Basing them on its own catalogue and Gareth's powerful imagination.'

In the rear-view mirror, Jack saw her flourish her version of the Visualiser.

'This must be the pair of Gareth's device. If I concentrate while I'm holding it, I can sense the other one. Similar to magnets, you know? The way like poles repel and opposite poles attract.' She closed her eyes. 'I can sense that he's close by.'

Jack flicked his eyes back to the road, saw that the car they were following had stopped. He had to brake sharply. Brigstocke spilled MonstaQuest cards into the footwell, and Toshiko jerked awake from her reverie.

The snaking trail of vehicles in front of them had completely halted. A chanting crowd of orange shirts milled along the street, completely blocking further progress. Three cars ahead, the driver was getting out and abandoning his vehicle.

'We're gonna have to walk,' Jack decided. 'Though we're never gonna beat these crowds.'

'Kick-off's not for another two hours,' Brigstocke said. 'If we cut down that alleyway over there, on foot, we can get in through the Press entrance.'

Jack unbuckled his seat belt. 'Let's do it. And Tosh, can

you delay the entry of the crowds into the Stadium? A bomb threat with a known code word?'

Brigstocke stared, appalled. 'Another pack of lies, Jack?'

Jack snorted. 'You think the truth is gonna help them?'

'If you keep this lot outside for too long, there'll be a riot!' snapped Brigstocke. 'And a bomb threat means the Press won't get in either.'

'We need the delay.'

Toshiko called from the back: 'I've put a spanner in the ticketing system. It'll read all valid tickets as forgeries, and jam the turnstiles. That should stall them. And it's early enough that they'll try and fix it before letting people in.' She started to switch off the computer. 'Oh, and I've put a judder in the Stadium's retractable roof, so now it can't decide whether it wants to open or close.'

'Attagirl.'

Jack put the SUV into lockdown, and the three of them squeezed out into the river of orange shirts. Almost at once, Toshiko was swept away from Jack and Brigstocke. They struggled against the tide of bodies, cutting across to try and rescue her. She was forced into the alleyway, but Jack and Brigstocke found they were dragged past it. Even above the excited babble of the crowd, Jack could hear Toshiko's scream for assistance.

'Gotta get back and help her!' Jack yelled. No way of reasoning with the surging stream of people, they were like a pack of animals herding down the roadway. The more he and Brigstocke struggled, the more the crowd surged, increasingly angry at their resistance. They managed to press themselves against the wall of a building, and edge back towards the alleyway.

Another scream from Toshiko cut off abruptly. There was

coarse laughter from the alley.

And then a blast of air that powered its way from the narrow entrance. Three orange-shirted bodies were flung above head height, out into the main street, accompanied by a shower of dirt and old newspapers. They fell onto the crowd, and rapidly dropped out of sight. A ripple of movement in the group where they'd landed suggested they were now receiving a kicking.

Jack got around the corner of the building as the gust of air died down again.

In the centre of the alleyway, all on her own, stood Toshiko. Jack ran to her. Her eyes were closed in concentration. In one hand she held the Visualiser, and in the other a MonstaQuest card. Jack touched her arm gently, and she opened her eyes.

'What happened?' he asked her.

'They were attacking me.'

'Looks like you handled it,' Jack said with an admiring tone.

'The Visualiser,' she explained. She revealed the face of her MonstaQuest card. It showed the roof lifting off a house, with the stark description: Gale. Toshiko looked uncertainly at Jack. 'I don't know whether I was controlling it, or it was controlling me. I just wanted them gone, and this huge squall picked them up and flung them aside.'

Brigstocke joined them, looking dishevelled. One pocket of his sports jacket was flapping and torn. 'We can get through this way to the Stadium,' he said. 'Look, you can see it straight ahead.' The skeletal towers loomed large in the distance. 'You know, I remember when they knocked down part of the old Cardiff Arms Park to build the Millennium Stadium.'

Jack chuckled. 'And I remember when they knocked down

all of the Cardiff Arms Hotel to build Cardiff Arms Park.'

'Don't be stupid,' said Brigstocke, 'that was in the nineteenth century.'

Jack indicated the Visualiser. 'Tosh, can you use it to tell us where Gareth is now?'

She closed her eyes to concentrate.

'Actually,' said Brigstocke, 'I don't think you need to bother.'

He was pointing down the alley towards the Millennium Stadium. Pouring through its roof into the dark evening sky was a dazzling column of green light.

TWENTY-THREE

A powerful transformation had overtaken the Millennium Stadium. Jack paused at the end of the players tunnel, and looked out onto the pitch.

Brigstocke was babbling next to him, to cover his nerves probably. 'I used to dream about walking down here. Running out on the pitch in front of a capacity crowd.'

'You wouldn't want a crowd here at the moment,' Toshiko told him. She stared anxiously into the ground. 'Are we too late, Jack?'

Gareth Portland stood in the centre circle, his head thrown back and his arms raised. A spiralling column of lime green light whirled like an inverted cone above him and up into the darkening sky. The roof was half-open, juddering backwards and forwards, undecided whether to enclose or release the force beneath. On the pitch, a bizarre assortment of MonstaQuest creatures capered around Gareth, churning up the turf with claws and hooves.

'I shoulda guessed he'd come here, Tosh,' murmured Jack. 'We've known since this place was constructed that it was aligned with the Rift.'

'What do you mean?' asked Brigstocke .

Jack looked at the journalist's baffled face, illuminated by the eerie green light. 'The playing surface was rotated through ninety degrees when they built the new Stadium.'

'How is this helping?' snarled Brigstocke, the fear starting to get to him. 'What are you suggesting we do to Gareth? Give him a feng shui blessing? Ring a bell and throw some sea salt and wave an incense stick around?'

Jack sighed. 'It's at times like this that I wish I could use one of those warheads we rescued from the Wanarian battle cruiser.'

Brigstocke gave him a sharp look. 'Is that possible?'

'There's an intergalactic treaty that strongly discourages it,' said Jack.

'Plus,' Toshiko explained, 'it would reduce Cardiff to a desert of polished glass.'

Brigstocke considered this for a second. 'That would be a bad thing?'

'You sound like you're not sure,' Toshiko told him.

Jack laughed. 'That's because he's from Swansea.' He took a few steps further into the Stadium, and the movement of air began to tug at his hair and coat. 'Hey, wait a minute…'

On the other side of the Stadium, three stewards in luminous jackets were moving from the North Stand and across the pitch. One shouted into his radio handset, while the other two ran ahead, gesturing and waving at Gareth.

'We gotta stop them,' snapped Jack, and raced out onto the grass. Toshiko and Brigstocke trailed behind.

Gareth tilted his head in the direction of the stewards. He lowered his left hand and, seconds later, a dazzling creature of fire and flame burst into life beside him. It scorched a burnt route across the turf.

'No!' yelled Jack to the gesticulating stewards as he pounded over the grass. 'Stay back!'

The fire creature fell upon the nearest two stewards. They barely had time to scream before they were consumed, their bodies flaring and vanishing in an instant. The fire exhausted itself, leaving two incinerated, smoking lumps on the blackened turf.

The third steward staggered to a halt, gaping in incredulity. Jack got to him, and dragged him, unprotesting, back to the touchline. Jack clutched the shocked man by the shoulders. 'You have to keep people away. Tell the police that Torchwood are handling this. You got that? Torchwood.'

The steward nodded dumbly.

'Don't let anyone out into the Stadium, because they'll die just like those first two. Stewards, police, staff, players – they all stay inside, understand?' Jack pushed the steward towards the exit tunnel. 'Especially Baldachi.'

The steward stumbled off, breaking into a run.

'Why Baldachi? Because he's key to this?' asked Brigstocke. 'Or because he's worth thirty million euro?'

'Because he's the cutest,' replied Jack. 'Have you seen him in those underwear advertisements?' He watched to see Brigstocke's reaction. It was important that the guy didn't zone out now, because that could put him and Torchwood in danger.

Brigstocke shook his head. 'You really know *nothing* about football, do you?'

'I have pockets of expertise,' said Jack defensively.

From the sideline they could see the vortex around Gareth was moving faster. A stiff breeze swirled around the Stadium. 'Where is Gareth getting the power from?' Brigstocke asked. 'You said he needed people's emotions, but there's no crowd.'

'Not yet.' Jack considered the steep rows of empty seats all around them. 'But boy, when they get here, it'll blow the roof off.'

'It's the Stadium's power!' said Toshiko. 'Look at those rows of floodlights in the roof. See how they're flickering? Gareth's drawing energy straight from the local grid. Like priming the pump, waiting for the crowds to arrive.'

Jack grinned at her, delighted. 'You're right! OK, Tosh, you need to get the satellite link disconnected and switch off the power.'

Toshiko was struggling with her PDA in one hand and the Visualiser device in the other. 'I need a schematic of the Stadium to locate the Press area. But I can't get a proper connection with all this background Rift activity.'

'I can show you!' Brigstocke's face was eager, excited.

'All right!' shouted Jack. 'I'll stay down here and keep Gareth's attention while you do that.'

As Toshiko and Brigstocke hurried back into the building, Jack began to pick his way cautiously over the springy turf. A motley collection of bizarre creatures danced attendance on Gareth. A scorpion creature arched its fat sting overhead, and snapped its enormous claws spasmodically. A couple of tall antelopes strutted back and forth, their snarling mouths full of drooling teeth. A broad-backed armadillo with a club tail scuttled in a short, angry circle.

Jack drew his revolver, wondering how close he'd need to be for a killing shot. His repaired ankle still throbbed as he stalked closer to the centre circle. It reminded him that he had to stay clear of anything that might completely devour him – even if that was survivable, it would take too long to recover.

Gareth hadn't noticed him yet. But something else had.

In the grass around him, double-headed flowers were bursting through the surface, like a stop-motion film of a plant lifecycle. Their heads reared, seeking him out, opening their petals and spitting at him. He flung up an arm to protect his face, and the dart-like seeds embedded themselves in his sleeve.

And in the heel of his hand.

He jumped back, stung. His gun-arm already felt numb. He was staggering away from the flowers, his balance abruptly deserting him. His head thumped down on the soft turf as the green light from the centre of the Stadium discoloured and faded and went to black.

Brigstocke said he'd been on enough Stadium tours and Press visits to the Millennium Stadium to know exactly where to find the controls for power and TV transmission. Toshiko was grateful that he hadn't withdrawn into a helpless, gibbering wreck in the face of the extraordinary events. Extraordinary for him, that was.

She attached remote control explosives to both the satellite uplink and the landline back-up, and keyed them so that she could activate them from her PDA. She would have preferred to run this from the equipment in the SUV, better still from her workstation back at the Hub. But they would be impossible to reach in time, so she had to improvise.

'Need to switch off the power next,' she told Brigstocke. The journalist didn't reply. She looked up from her handiwork on the TV equipment, and saw that he had slipped through a nearby door.

'Mr Brigstocke? David?'

She pushed the door open and found him in one of the

Press boxes. The angled windows offered a magnificent outlook over the whole ground.

Brigstocke wasn't admiring the view, though. He was facing away from the window, with his hand to his mouth in shock. He barely moved, though Toshiko could hear him taking little panicky breaths.

There were other people in the Press box. Some of them were seated at the commentary positions, others stood looking out over the Stadium. But they were all stock-still. Unblinking statues. Living dead men.

Toshiko heard a soft scraping sound from the window, like a wiper dragged over a dry windscreen. There were two lizards clinging to the outside of the glass, chirruping as they traversed the window with their toe pads. One of them lazily licked its eye with a long grey tongue.

Brigstocke abruptly leaped across the room and twisted Toshiko away from the window. 'Don't look at them!' he hissed. 'I remember them from the cards I saw in the car.' He pulled a handful of MonstaQuest cards from his jacket pocket, and shuffled through them with frightened fingers. 'There, see!' He brandished one in front of her eyes. 'Gorgon Gekko.' Brigstocke uttered a brittle laugh. 'Funny when you first read it.' He noticed Toshiko was trying to compare the cartoon image with the real creatures. 'No! Don't look at them!' He ushered her from the room, back into the access corridor. 'The text explains that they can freeze enemies into immobility, if they make eye contact for long enough.'

'That's not plausible,' she told him.

'Well, tell that to those journalists in there,' Brigstocke shouted at her.

Toshiko looked at the card again. 'This must be one that Gareth invented. But he's actually brought it to life.' She grabbed the door handle. 'We have to see what else he's doing.'

'Not from that Press box,' Brigstocke told her. 'Try one further down.'

This new Press box was also full of blankly staring journalists. One was halfway through biting into a sandwich. Another was poised with his fingers in mid air above a laptop computer. When Brigstocke spotted a third one with a half-full glass of champagne lifted to his lips, he smacked it out of the man's frozen hands.

Toshiko hurried over to him in concern. 'What's the matter?'

'It's Ieuan Walters, the bastard!' Brigstocke looked furious. 'Wait till I see Eleri. Mid-Wales Beer Festival, my arse! He's glugging champagne at the international, the crafty sod.'

Toshiko moved cautiously to the front of the room. 'No lizards clinging to these windows,' she noted with relief.

'They must have made their way along the row,' Brigstocke suggested.

Toshiko looked down onto the pitch. The tiered seats dropped away towards the pitch in a vertiginous slope. At the centre of the ground, Gareth still dominated the scene with his bizarre alien courtiers.

Brigstocke spread the MonstaQuest cards on the desk in front of him, and began to pick out the creatures he could see.

'We can't let this get out,' Toshiko said. She called up the control interface on her PDA, and set off the remote explosives. The satellite feed and the landline severed instantly. Monitors across the Stadium fizzed into white noise or colour bars. With another remote command from the PDA, she began to shut the Stadium roof.

The green vortex around Gareth faltered, playing out on the closing roof like a strange laser show.

Gareth had noticed what was happening. He rotated in a full circle, as though scanning the entire Stadium with his baleful gaze, until coming to a halt and pointing.

Even at this distance, Toshiko could see what he was doing. With a thrill of horror, she saw that he was pointing straight at her.

A pair of bat-black nightmare creatures flapped their dreadful wings and began to swoop across the Stadium towards the Press box.

Jack whooped in air as he came back to life.

Poison was a tricky one in his long experience of death and resurrection. If it stayed in the system, it kept killing him, and revival was a multi-stage affair. If he was able to metabolise it, like now, his recovery was swift.

Two fat birds, savage crows the size of Rottweilers, were pecking at the sleeve of his coat. He rolled over, but couldn't shake them off. So he retrieved the Webley revolver from the grass, and took off the birds' heads with a couple of shots.

Jack tapped his earcomm. 'Tosh, how are you getting on?' The hiss of static told him that no signal was getting through.

Gareth was thirty metres away, and apparently engrossed with something way up in the stands. Jack took careful aim at the back of the man's head. He was applying first pressure to the trigger when he felt a fresh tug on his coat. A flock of the Rottweiler-crows seized his clothes, flesh, and hair in their talons, and lifted him bodily into the air.

Jack couldn't angle the Webley to hit any of them. The ground vanished beneath him at dizzying speed, and he was soon carried high up above the middle tier of seats. Now wouldn't be a good time to struggle free, he decided.

The monstrous birds had other ideas. As they swooped over the stand, they released him. Jack flailed in mid air, as though there might be something to grab on to. The last thing he saw was a balcony filled with padded chairs and a sliding door made of plate glass before he smashed into the stands.

The hideous bat-creatures slammed onto the Press box's window again. A faint trace of lines spread over the surface of the glass. Brigstocke shrank back against the far wall. 'We have to get out of here.'

'No,' said Toshiko in a firm, level tone. 'We have to be able to see what's happening in the Stadium.'

Down on the pitch, an enormous crevasse was opening up. Gareth Portland stood on a column of earth, a spindly tower that poked precariously up and supported him in the middle of the maelstrom. Fat jungle vines spewed from the dark earth and over the grass, snaking off in search of the stands. The thick boles of gnarled trees reared up from the green turf, and their branches whipped around in the tearing wind that circled the inside of the Stadium.

'What does Gareth think he's doing?' moaned Brigstocke.

'There is no Gareth any more,' Toshiko explained. 'The Visualiser is completely controlling him. Turning this place into an alien world. From here, it'll spread out across Cardiff.'

The bat-creatures smacked into the glass, cracking the glass and smearing fresh spittle from their foam-flecked jaws.

'Those things are going to open this box like a packed

lunch,' yelled Brigstocke. 'Can't you cut off the Stadium power? Won't that stop him?'

'It'll only stop him generating new creatures,' said Toshiko. She brushed something from her face, and found that shards of glass had cut her cheek and palm. 'Besides, I have a much better idea. And I need your help.'

Jack resurrected in a mess of glass and blood. He had fallen to his death into one of the private boxes on the Stadium's middle tier. He struggled up, and surveyed the arena. Either he'd been dead for a while this time, or things had moved on faster than he'd expected.

The retractable roof was fully closed, reflecting back the shimmer of green light that now infused the whole building. A tangle of strange foliage sprawled over the entire pitch, through which sprouted a forest of extraterrestrial trees. Fantastical creatures crawled and galloped in an alien landscape. And at its centre, Gareth conducted events from a thin podium of green turf within a ravine that cut deep into the earth below the Stadium.

Gareth was directing his attention in the direction of the Press gallery. Jack snatched up a pair of binoculars from the private box, and focused them upwards.

He could just make out Toshiko and Brigstocke in the window of the far Press box, grappling with the Visualiser device. A flock of the Rottweiler-crows and a couple of bat-creatures were hurling themselves repeatedly at the cracked glass in a desperate attempt to reach them.

The ground shook like an earthquake. Jack snapped his head back towards the pitch. He blinked in disbelief. Struggling out of the further reach of the crevasse in the pitch was an enormous humanoid shape, its bald white skull fringed with a halo of curly red hair. The hands were bulbous, and when it placed its elbows on the edge of the ravine, it revealed it was wearing yellow-striped dungarees.

The creature threw back its pale white face, and beneath the bulbous red nose was a mouth filled with daggers.

'A killer clown.' Jack bellowed with laughter. 'That has gotta be Tosh!' She must have inserted herself in the game using the other Visualiser. She was giving Gareth a fight. But there was surely no way that she could win against the guy who *created* MonstaQuest?

The clown had pulled itself free now. Gareth directed his monsters to attack the bizarre newcomer. Even the alien trees rippled and began to shuffle forward to defend their creator.

Jack surveyed the rest of the Stadium. The howling wind that encircled the enclosed space was beginning to loosen chairs and hoardings. But soaring towards him from the stand beyond the goalposts was another extraordinary sight. A flying unicorn.

The pale white coat was dappled green in the supernatural light. It seemed to toss its head at him as it approached. Jack clambered up onto the balcony rail, waited for the amazing creature to pass, and leaped onto its back.

He almost overshot. But the animal dropped its shoulder and swung around so that Jack was able to rebalance.

He sat well forward on the animal's withers, plunging his hands into its silky mane and pushing his legs over the point of the shoulder to keep them clear of the elegantly beating wings. He held on grimly as it veered into the wind and out over the centre of the Stadium.

The unicorn shimmied right a little, then swooped through a sudden squall in the wind. Its legs kicked away the snatching branches of the alien trees as the hooves skimmed the canopy. Gareth Portland was straight ahead, facing away on his tall thin pedestal, his red hair glowing in the unnatural light. Trees and animals blurred past Jack's face. He grappled with his flapping coat as he retrieved the Webley.

'Hey, Gareth!' he bellowed into the wind.

Gareth twisted around to see the unicorn approaching.

'Game over!' yelled Jack, and loosed off a single shot that took Gareth smack in the forehead.

The man's head snapped back, and he dropped wordlessly into the alien abyss. Jack watched the Vandrogonite Visualiser spinning end over end as it tumbled after him.

The tornado in the Stadium howled, paused, and changed direction. The gruesome creatures scrabbled for purchase with hooves and claws and hands as the shifting alien surface slid towards the dark maw that had just consumed Gareth and the Visualiser. It was like a tablecloth was pulled into a hole at the centre of the pitch, dragging everything helplessly down with it.

Jack flew up towards the Press box. The monstrous bats and the Rottweiler-crows were abruptly snatched backwards, as though propelled from a gun, and hurled into the centre of the Stadium. The unicorn circled around in front of the cracked glass of the Press box, and Jack could make out Toshiko and Brigstocke clutching the other Visualiser between their outstretched hands. They turned to grin back at Jack. Brigstocke let go of the Visualiser and gave Jack a double thumbs-up gesture.

Which was the exact moment that the unicorn vanished, and sent Jack plummeting to the stands far below.

* * *

Toshiko was mopping his brow when Jack revived this

time. He found that he was badly twisted across a couple of Stadium seats. Brigstocke sat several rows further up the tier, shaking his head in disbelief.

Toshiko directed Jack's attention to the bowl of the Stadium. There was an ominous cracking noise from his spine when he straightened up to take a look.

In the stark white of the floodlights, it was clear that the crevasse had disappeared. There was no trace of the alien flora or fauna, though the turf was rutted and torn, and chairs and hoardings were strewn across its surface.

He looked at Toshiko's scratched, blood-flecked face. She looked exhausted, but pleased. 'Well played, Tosh,' smiled Jack.

Toshiko pulled out her PDA and tapped something into it. The giant scoreboard flickered into life. Jack looked up and laughed. It said: 'Torchwood 1, Achenbrite 0'.

TWENTY-FOUR

Toshiko was delighted with her 'Get Well' card. Owen had knocked up a design based on the MonstaQuest pack, with her picture square and centre. The monster type was 'Genius', and she had high scores for all the attributes: 'Intelligence', 'Imagination', 'Bravery'.

Typical Toshiko, she'd quibbled why they'd only rated her nine out of ten for 'Dress Sense'.

'You're making a fuss about nothing, anyway,' she said. 'I've only got a few glass cuts on my face. You should have seen what happened to Jack.'

'Get Well Soon cards are wasted on Jack,' noted Owen.

'Perhaps we should get him a Get Well Slowly card,' Ianto said. He and Gwen had just clattered in through the cog-wheel door, returning from their hunt for the guerrilla gorilla. 'He might take a bit of time off.'

'Careful, Ianto.' Gwen patted him on the shoulder. 'You're starting to sound like Rhys. I'm just off the phone from him, and he's all "you're late again, Gwen". No thank you for warning him to stay away from the Stadium, mind.'

'Was he angry about missing the match?' asked Ianto.

'Angrier that Banana got pissed in the City Arms and had to be carried home.'

Jack hung back quietly, unnoticed. He enjoyed the easy confidence that his team had together, friendship and trust forged in combat against whatever the Rift could throw at them. Sometimes he just liked to watch them like this, so proud of their achievements.

He left them in the Hub celebrating, and slipped away for his appointment in town. David Brigstocke was already sitting at a table in the window of Casa Celi when Jack arrived.

'My first instinct was that this would be a trick.' Brigstocke tried to sound nonchalant, but Jack could practically hear his heart hammering the inside of his tweed jacket. Did the guy have nothing else in his wardrobe? 'Are you humouring me, Jack?'

Jack pushed aside a red napkin containing cutlery so that he could lean on the table. 'Stand you up? Never.'

Brigstocke put his hand into his jacket pocket.

'No recording, please,' said Jack.

'Would there be any point?'

Jack shook his head very slightly. 'But tonight, I'm trusting you. Let's just talk.'

Brigstocke brought his hand back out again, and folded it over the other on the metal table. 'I notice that you walked here.'

'Exercise is how I retain these irresistible good looks.'

'Something more than that, I think.' Brigstocke's eyes glittered. 'Your foot's completely healed. Impossibly fast, wouldn't you say? And as for the injuries you sustained in the Stadium…'

Jack beckoned the waiter over and ordered a glass of iced

water for himself and a Morreti beer for Brigstocke.

'Captain Hark-a-ness!' declared the waiter. 'And-a what-a else can I get-a for you?'

Jack grinned and sent him on his way. He knew that Enrico Celi was a Welsh Italian with a natural South Wales accent. 'Save it for the punters, Rico,' he laughed.

Rico winked, and returned to a large table at the rear of the café. A small group of Italians from the international were trying to enjoy themselves. Depending on the result, Rico had been planning either a celebration or a wake, but the match postponement had dampened enthusiasm. A smaller number had turned up than he'd expected. Jack studied them across the room as they gazed sullenly at their gnocchi. All of them had the dark hair and tan that made even the meanest of features look attractive. Well, compared to the Welsh anyway, thought Jack as one drunk hammered on the front window while staggering past.

Which brought his attention back to Brigstocke.

'*I saw that one of its heads seemed to have had a fatal wound,*' Brigstocke quoted, '*but that this deadly injury had healed and the whole world had marvelled and followed the beast.*'

'Beast?' smiled Jack. 'I've been called that before.'

Brigstocke leaned closer. 'It's from the Bible. In the church this morning, do you remember? You're not a beast, Jack. But you're something more than human.'

Jack sipped his water and said nothing.

'And I've seen you and your team in action today. Properly, I mean. Saving all those people. And so much more. I hope I helped.'

Jack thought about the unicorn. 'More than you know.'

'What will all those people know about this?'

'Not much,' admitted Jack. The rest of the Torchwood team

had swung into action in the Stadium aftermath. The football players got Retcon added to their team-room drinks. And the recuperating TV crews and stewards received particular treatment from a special ambulance crew made up of Ianto, Gwen and Owen.

Brigstocke wasn't convinced. 'How do you explain the wreck of the Stadium?'

'Nasty bit of vandalism,' suggested Jack. 'Freak winds.'

'And that light show in the night sky?'

'Good idea,' smiled Jack. 'Light show. Hadn't thought of that.'

Brigstocke scowled. 'You're just giving them a pack of lies.'

'People want to believe it,' Jack said. 'They wouldn't believe the truth. There's no point having the facts if you can't process them and stay sane.' He contemplated the water in his glass as he swirled it around. 'Knowledge isn't the same as wisdom.'

'Why? What's the difference?'

Jack smiled. 'Knowledge is when you can tell that a tomato is a fruit. Wisdom is when you leave it out of a fruit salad.'

The journalist blinked slowly, unsure about this.

'I know you want to join Torchwood.' Jack was pleased to see that Brigstocke's pupils dilated at this. 'But would that be wise?'

Brigstocke clearly took this as encouragement. 'I want to be a proper part of it. Not just because I'm chasing down what happened to Rhodri—'

'But because you got a taste of it today, yeah.' Jack looked out through the café window, into the evening. The pavement tables were occupied by a hardy bunch of inveterate smokers, huddled against the cold, suffering for their addiction.

'Torchwood work hard to protect these people. And just as hard to prevent them knowing they're being protected. We can't always save everyone.' He stared back at Brigstocke. 'We couldn't save Rhodri.'

And Jack explained how Brigstocke's friend had been a victim of a Weevil attack. Who Torchwood were. Why they'd covered up the death. Brigstocke seemed to relax into his seat, as though the revelations had confirmed everything he'd always believed. To conclude his explanation, Jack stuck his leg out beside the table and performed an ankle rotation with his completely healed foot.

'Do you still want to join Torchwood?'

Brigstocke was good. He gave the impression that he was thinking carefully before he said: 'Yes, Jack. Yes, I do.'

'Your turn, David,' Jack murmured. 'Tell me what you already know. How you discovered it. Who told you.'

Brigstocke did just that. Jack listened openly, uncritically, for nearly an hour while the Italian table cleared and Rico brought them more drinks. Sometimes Jack peered at things through the big glass window beside them – the straggling remnants of the international, staggering through the town centre and in danger of missing their last train home. Or giggling kids in lurid Halloween costumes, toting bags of booty from their trick-or-treating. But mostly he looked candidly into Brigstocke's earnest, pleading eyes, gauging the journalist's pain and passion.

'OK,' Jack concluded. He gulped down the dregs of his latest glass of water. 'I'm gonna talk to the others.'

The last of the Halloween kids brushed past the café window, squeaking the plastic tip of his devil's pitchfork along the glass.

Trick or treat, Jack thought.

'Let me sleep on it, David. And I'll contact you again tomorrow.'

By then, the Retcon in the journalist's last Morreti beer would have done the trick. David would forget he'd ever been interested in Torchwood. Jack knew it was so much easier to hide the truth than have to tell Brigstocke a pack of lies.

Acknowledgements

Albert DePetrillo, for the opportunity.

Steve Tribe and Gary Russell, for knowledge and wisdom.

James Goss and Phil Ford, for the company.

Lee Binding, for the cover.

Michael Stevens, Joe Lidster, John Barrowman and Anna Lea, for the audiobook of *Another Life*.

Anne Summerfield, for always.

TORCHWOOD
THE TWILIGHT STREETS
Gary Russell

ISBN 978 1 846 07439 4
UK £6.99 US$11.99/$14.99 CDN

There's a part of the city that no one much goes to, a collection of rundown old houses and gloomy streets. No one stays there long, and no one can explain why – something's not quite right there.

Now the Council is renovating the district, and a new company is overseeing the work. There will be street parties and events to show off the newly gentrified neighbourhood: clowns and face-painters for the kids, magicians for the adults – the street entertainers of Cardiff, out in force.

None of this is Torchwood's problem. Until Toshiko recognises the sponsor of the street parties: Bilis Manger.

Now there is something for Torchwood to investigate. But Captain Jack Harkness has never been able to get into the area; it makes him physically ill to go near it. Without Jack's help, Torchwood must face the darker side of urban Cardiff alone…

Featuring Captain Jack Harkness as played by John Barrowman, with Gwen Cooper, Owen Harper, Toshiko Sato and Ianto Jones as played by Eve Myles, Burn Gorman, Naoki Mori and Gareth David-Lloyd, in the hit series created by Russell T Davies for BBC Television.

TORCHWOOD
SKYPOINT
Phil Ford

ISBN 978 1 846 07575 9
UK £6.99 US$11.99/$14.99 CDN

'If you're going to be anyone in Cardiff, you're going to be at SkyPoint!'

SkyPoint is the latest high-rise addition to the ever-developing Cardiff skyline. It's the most high-tech, avant-garde apartment block in the city. And it's where Rhys Williams is hoping to find a new home for himself and Gwen. Gwen's more concerned by the money behind the tower block – Besnik Lucca, a name she knows from her days in uniform.

When Torchwood discover that residents have been going missing from the tower block, one of the team gets her dream assignment. Soon SkyPoint's latest newly married tenants are moving in. And Toshiko Sato finally gets to make a home with Owen Harper.

Then something comes out of the wall…

Featuring Captain Jack Harkness as played by John Barrowman, with Gwen Cooper, Owen Harper, Toshiko Sato and Ianto Jones as played by Eve Myles, Burn Gorman, Naoki Mori and Gareth David-Lloyd, in the hit series created by Russell T Davies for BBC Television.

TORCHWOOD
ALMOST PERFECT
James Goss

ISBN 978 1 846 07573 5
UK £6.99 US$11.99/$14.99 CDN

Emma is 30, single and frankly desperate. She woke up this morning with nothing to look forward to but another evening of unsuccessful speed-dating. But now she has a new weapon in her quest for Mr Right. And it's made her almost perfect.

Gwen Cooper woke up this morning expecting the unexpected. As usual. She went to work and found a skeleton at a table for two and a colleague in a surprisingly glamorous dress. Perfect.

Ianto Jones woke up this morning with no memory of last night. He went to work, where he caused amusement, suspicion and a little bit of jealousy. Because Ianto Jones woke up this morning in the body of a woman. And he's looking just about perfect.

Jack Harkness has always had his doubts about Perfection.

Featuring Captain Jack Harkness as played by John Barrowman, with Gwen Cooper and Ianto Jones as played by Eve Myles and Gareth David-Lloyd, in the hit series created by Russell T Davies for BBC Television.

Also available from BBC Books

THE
TORCHWOOD
ARCHIVES

ISBN 978 1 846 07459 2
£14.99

Separate from the Government
Outside the police
Beyond the United Nations…

Founded by Queen Victoria in 1879, the Torchwood Institute has long battled against alien threats to the British Empire. The Torchwood Archives is an insider's look into the secret world of this unique investigative team.

In-depth background on personnel, case files on alien enemies of the Crown and descriptions of extra-terrestrial technology collected over the years will uncover more about the world of Torchwood than ever previously known, including some of the biggest mysteries surrounding the Rift in space and time running through Cardiff.

Based on the hit series
created by Russell T Davies
for BBC Television.